He's chari.
Neither wants

She took another bite and moaned. Cowboy's blood ran south, and he shifted in his seat. His sweatpants were not much help in hiding his excitement over being near her.

She had crumbs on her face from the bite. "You have some"—Cowboy pointed to a spot on his face—"here." He about died when she stuck out her tongue and slowly licked the area. He knew she wasn't trying to be sexy, but dammit, she had been.

After she missed the spot, he reached over with his thumb. "Here." He wiped the piece of cobbler from her cheek.

She surprised him by grabbing his hand, putting his thumb in her mouth, and sucking off the dessert. A thrill of anticipation leapt up his spine.

He groaned. "Good God, LizzyBeth, you're killing me." He stood, leaned over, and helped her stand. Pulling her close, he said, "I'm going to do something I've wanted to do since I met you." He leaned in and touched his lips to hers, gently molding their mouths together.

He had wanted this woman in his arms since she had shown up on his doorstep with her toolbox. Now, he had her in his arms and willing. But how ready was she? When she put her arms around his neck, he darted his tongue in her mouth and moaned. A passionate kiss was one thing, but sex was another.

Cowboy rubbed his hands up and down her back, pulling her as close as possible so he could feel her unbound breasts mold against his chest. He explored her mouth with his tongue, eliciting a moan from her. Good God, his cock was hard for her.

Knowing if he didn't stop now he would drag her to his bed all caveman-like, he pulled back from her. Her closed eyes fluttered open, and raw desire pooled in them.

"I think I'd best stop now before I do something you aren't ready for."

Titles by Sheila Kell

AFTERNOON DELIGHT

AN AGENTS OF HIS NOVEL

SHEILA KELL

*Cunningham
Publishing*

Afternoon Delight

Copyright @ 2022 by Sheila Kell

ISBN (Print): 9781957587004

ISBN (EBook): 9781957587011

Dedication

To Dianne Hawkins
You're the best friend a girl could want. Thanks for
your continued support in life and this endeavor.

Acknowledgments

Writing Cowboy's story was one of the funnest books I've researched and written. Who knew cowboys were so fun? While I used a real town in Texas, I imagined all the rest.

A special thanks goes to my beta readers: my mother, Dawn Stanton Tohill, Cheryl McCullough, Helen McNabb, Jessica Neuhart, Barbara Tolf Williams, and Devorah Bergman, all gave it a good read before I submitted it to Hot Tree Editing where Virginia and the Hot Tree team did a fabulous job helping me finalize this novella.

I'm excited to have found another Eric Battershell Photography original for the cover photo. Welcome David Wills to the ranks of the HIS men.

As always, I thank you, the reader, for your support in reading my books. You are the reason I do what I do.

1

MIKE "COWBOY" VAUGHN enjoyed blowing things up more than anything else. He twitched his lips with a suppressed smile—scratch that. Working with munitions ranked second best because nothing beat sliding between a woman's soft thighs.

"I saw that," Danny Franks, call sign Ballpark, whispered over his radio. "He's smiling. Boss," he called to their team leader, Ken Patrick, "he's having way too much fun. Let's hope there aren't any bombs to diffuse. He might cream his pants right in front of us."

Cowboy bristled. With the explosives he made, he knew the risks. When someone else created an explosive, the stakes were high. Something could go wrong, and when it went wrong with explosives, it really went wrong. "Shut it," he ground out to Ballpark.

He almost chuckled at that call sign. Danny used to just be called Franks. Danny had been a DEA agent, so he had no military special ops call sign. When the two men were together, a Ball Park Franks commercial came on, and that was what Danny had brought to grill, so Cowboy began calling him that. It hadn't taken long for everyone to join in the harassment.

"Son of a—"

"Language, Ballpark," Boss interrupted, his voice vibrating with intensity. Ever since Boss had adopted a son, he had changed his tune on language. Yet, that also meant it was time to stop the joking they used to release tension. It was time for steel focus, and Cowboy especially needed to use it since he held life or death in his hands.

Ignoring his teammates, he confirmed his charges were perfect on the hinges for a controlled explosion, then backed away from the metal door and voiced, "Fire in the hole." Without a moment's hesitation, he blew open a place to breach the concrete building where they were attempting to rescue three hostages.

Six HIS agents joined the op—Boss, Ballpark, Doc, Cowboy, all from Alpha team, and Romeo and Speedy from Bravo team. Their brief intel led them to believe they would encounter three, maybe four, tangos—terrorists—who held three kidnapped women, and HIS had the odds.

Piece of cake.

Or it would have been had they been able to acquire building plans. With time being of the essence, they would fly blind inside the new structure.

Boss tossed a smoke grenade into the building.

Before Cowboy could jinx their op—yes, he believed in some things that made no sense—he put his gas mask on and pulled his M4 Carbine to his shoulder, then followed his team leader into the unknown situation with smoke everywhere. Boss went left with Speedy and Ballpark, and Cowboy went right with Romeo and Doc. The two teams were to sweep the building, take out the tangos, and rescue the three female hostages.

Once they turned down a hallway, a shot hit him squarely in the chest. His breath caught, and the pain surprised him as red seeped on his black shirt. He collapsed on the ground, knowing Doc couldn't help him until the hostages were safe. He attempted to point his M4 at the threat around his teammates but knew it was hopeless. *Is this how my life will end?* He would die saving someone if that was what it took. Sure, noble of him, and the chicks dug that type of talk. But he didn't want to die because he had been stupid. *Why hadn't I paid more attention to my surroundings?*

Inside the building, their rescue resembled a Charlie Foxtrot—clusterfuck. As for his team, most had a smattering of some foreign language, primarily Spanish. Yet, he could understand the foreign words that were probably Eastern European without knowing for sure.

"Drop your weapons or she dies." Every tango holding a gun to the head of a hostage said that.

Fuck. Fuck. Fuck. Romeo only took a second to step forward as team leader for their split element. He also yelled for the tangos to "Put down your weapons." Of course, it did no good. They were at a stalemate.

By God, if I'm going to die, my men had best save the hostages, was all he could think while lying there. His death had to be worth something. It had to matter in the end.

3

Wearing gas masks, Jake Cavanaugh along with Jesse, AJ, and Brad Hamilton held three faux hostages, who pretended they were not wearing gas masks by coughing and acting as if the smoke had bothered them. They were the bosses' wives, who'd volunteered to be in the action. Kate Hamilton almost didn't count because she had been FBI, Megan Hamilton was a newspaper reporter, and Madison Hamilton was a former supermodel. Still, the women knew how to take care of themselves, so seeing them play damsels in distress made him want to laugh.

Jake screamed in Spanish—yeah, that sounded threatening.

Cowboy could do nothing but pretend to be mortally wounded. Sure, he'd had a vest on, so he technically could've survived, but in their games, a chest shot put you out and made you the medic's problem. Only Doc couldn't deal with him because the hostages were in danger, and he was Romeo's only backup.

Jake continued to shout at Romeo and Doc, who refused to drop their weapons even though Jake held a gun to Kate's head. From the sideline, Cowboy watched Kate try to get Romeo's attention with her eyes, and she kept dropping them like any trained operative would if they meant to fall and free up the target.

They got lucky in the hostage Jake chose; her faux background for the exercise had been law enforcement, so she knew what to expect.

Where were Boss and the others? Had they been shot also, or were they lost? Maybe the team would get lucky and they had planned a surprise attack from behind. Anything was possible, and Cowboy had to fucking sit on the sidelines and watch. *Stupid. Stupid.* He had been an idiot by not paying enough attention. He had been thinking of getting home. His injury meant a longer debrief on what not to do.

In the next instant, Kate dropped, and Romeo shot Jake. Doc shot Jesse. And two shots rang out from the hallways, catching the other two Hamilton brothers. Four tangos down. The agents rushed forward and pushed weapons out of the way of the tangos, then patted them down for more weapons and explosives. "Safety first" had been a motto Cowboy didn't always adhere to, and that was why he was dying while the others saved the day.

"EndEx. EndEx," Jesse shouted, stopping the exercise. "Pick up your wounded, and let's get inside to debrief."

Ha. Ha. Ha. Yet, Cowboy was the only one wounded on the good side. Doc hadn't even had time to check on him, and he could have been dead by now. He called himself an idiot again.

The debrief went as expected. Cowboy was razzed and used as a "what not to do" in that situation. He just hadn't been fast enough. He had seen the tango, but the tango had seen him first. The tangos had been waiting for him. The HIS agents had tripped something outside the building, and the explosion had only prepared the tangos for them. With the tangos knowing standard special ops tactics, they had donned gas masks to be ready for anything. Just their fucking luck to have smart tangos.

5

After a quick shower, Cowboy said, "I've got to run. My handyman will be waiting."

"What have you done? Has the whole place been rebuilt?" Ballpark asked. "You've had the handyman working for a couple of months now. Is there something we should know?"

Cowboy rolled his eyes. "I've just had some remodeling done, that's all."

Doc teased, "I think you're crushing on your handyman and making up things for him to do."

"What's he like? Can I meet him?" Speedy asked, always on the prowl. He didn't hide his sexual preference, and no one cared either way. They were teammates and family.

"No, and hell no." Cowboy left the locker room and headed home. He had purchased an older home that needed remodeling. He had planned to do the work himself, but HIS had kept him busier than expected. He had found Howe Handy to help with a leaky pipe. When the owner had said they did remodel, he decided to give them a shot. He had been pleasantly surprised by the quality of work and decided to use them for the remaining remodel.

After he parked his truck on the street, he settled his cowboy hat on his head and walked to the front door of his home. Excitement wove through him. Today, he would see his newly finished bathroom. He had been trusting and hadn't peeked at the work whilst in progress.

His handyman, with a black metal toolbox, stood waiting. If only the guys knew the truth about his handyman, they would go nuts. He would never live it down.

He grinned. His upset at dying during the exercise faded. "Hello, LizzyBeth."

2

IT HAD BEEN two months since Elizabeth Howe had met Cowboy. He insisted on calling her LizzyBeth, so she'd given up explaining her name was Elizabeth. As a client, Cowboy kept her busy doing things she figured he could do. Whether Cowboy did it because he was too busy, did not want to do the work, or because he felt sorry for her as a woman in the profession, she didn't care. Work was work, and she needed the pay.

"Hi, Cowboy," she responded. "How was work today?"

"Oh, you know. I blew up a door, killed some bad guys, all in a day's work." He winked at her. He did that a lot—winked and flirted.

Her ex-husband had never winked at her, but she had seen him wink at other women. She had fallen in love with Sean, and they had quickly married. Things had gone well for them until she found out he had another woman. He had asked for forgiveness, and she had stupidly granted it. She then found out months later he had cheated again, paying another woman's rent.

Elizabeth had left him the next day and filed for divorce. Sean had let her have everything, which consisted of a home mortgaged to the hilt and a handyman business that had been failing since he had been screwing around more than working. Yet, she had worked hard to revive Howe Handy.

Not everyone would allow a woman handyman. That darn guy pride lost her clients. She had managed to get the business into the black and make a dent in the debt she and Sean had split.

Sean admitted that he had been stupid and screwed up the best thing that had happened to him. He wanted them to be a family again, but she wasn't fool enough to trust him again. He had been just like her father and her late brother. The men had been all sweet and loving one moment, only for her to find out they were two-timing cheaters and liars to boot. Her friends told her all men were not like that, but all the men in her life had been. Either she was a magnet for cheaters, or her friends lied to save face on their relationships.

Which meant Cowboy was like the others—a flirt and a cheat. No man believed in forever when it pertained to wedding vows. Her dad had not, and her husband had not. Something about Cowboy, though, made her think he was harmless. She couldn't pinpoint what it was that gave her that feeling.

"I'll be done finishing up the bathroom renovation today." She had renovated his guest bathroom, and she had done a spectacular job of it. Elizabeth worked hard to incorporate the client's wishes with style and class. On this project, Cowboy had given her free rein. She had taken in the rest of how he had decorated and made a room she knew he would love.

"You haven't looked yet, have you?" she asked. They had made a deal that it would be a total surprise for Cowboy, with no peeking while she wasn't there.

"One hundred percent no peeking," he assured her.

She didn't know whether to believe him or not, but it didn't matter. She needed a few hours to hang the mirror, clean the mud from the backsplash surrounding the tub, and caulk around everything. It would be an easy day—finally payday. She had struggled a bit without this payment. He had always offered to pay her as she went, but she refused. In no way would she allow someone to pay her for work she hadn't completed. It was just a rule she had learned early. She never settled for partial service, and she never wanted to be paid for any partial service.

"Hurry up, then," Cowboy said. "I can't wait to see it." He went to the fridge and grabbed a beer. "Want anything?"

She shook her head. "No, I'm good." She'd brought water because it was free and good for the body. "Let me finish up, and I'll be out in no time."

"All right." He had moved to the couch and had the remote in his hand. He had dismissed her to do her work, and she liked that about him. He wasn't chatting at the beginning of her workday, only at the end when he began the flirting again.

Elizabeth took two hours in the bathroom and, after wiping everything down and cleaning the floors, decided it was ready for the owner of the house to see the finished product.

With the friendship the two had sort of created with her working for him so long, she was able to tease him into closing his eyes and allowing her to guide him to the bathroom. She wouldn't admit it out loud, but she enjoyed touching the firm muscles on his arms as she helped him find his way to the room.

"You're not going to run me into a wall, are you?" he joked.

"That depends on whether you like it or not," she joked back. She halted Cowboy's progress forward. "Okay, open your eyes." Her heart pounded like it did every time a client saw her final work. Would they like it? Would they fire her and not pay her? So many questions and emotions, from giddy to worried, sprang through her system.

He turned, taking in the complete room. "Wow. This is amazing." He turned back to her. "Woman, you are worth every penny. I love it."

Excitement filled her body. In the past, when Cowboy was like that, it meant a bonus, and she liked perks just as much as when someone loved her work. The two went hand in hand. She still had plenty of debt to worry about, so this payday would be beneficial.

"Now," he said, "I've been thinking of updating my kitchen. Nothing too fancy, just updating some of the cabinets, adding a backsplash, then upgrading the appliances."

Desire, not the romantic kind, ran through her. She

had wanted to get her hands on Cowboy's kitchen from the moment she had seen it. It wasn't old-fashioned, but it had so much potential. "As in repainting the cabinets or replacing them?" She hoped for a mix of both.

"I'm not sure. What would you do if it was yours?" Cowboy asked as he led her back to the kitchen area.

She loved and hated that question, but with Cowboy, love worked easier because his style wasn't far off hers. "I'd stain them and add some glass doors. Over here"—she gestured to the shelves to the right of the sink—"I'd tear these down and make open shelves." She waited to see if he agreed with her or saw her vision.

Cowboy nodded. "I can see it. Good. Go forward. You can start as early as tomorrow because I'll be home all day."

She took a moment to thank God for another job right after the last one. She hadn't had anything lined up, and it had worried her. What would she do when Cowboy ran out of things to renovate or fix? He had been her best customer since she took over the business alone.

"I'll be here. Let me get a few measurements today."

He nodded, so she went to her toolbox and took out a notepad, pencil, and tape measure. As she measured the cabinets she wanted to replace with glass, Cowboy began the "after work" talking and flirting. She enjoyed the time, especially since she didn't make time to spend with friends as much as she wanted.

"Do you want to watch the game with me tomorrow?"

She preferred working, but she didn't want to offend him. "How about I watch it while I work?"

"Darlin'," he said. She loved the drawl he used when he said it. "You can do anything you want while you're here."

That was when she began to wonder if working for Cowboy was more pleasure than business.

3

IT WAS THE first college baseball game Cowboy had watched alone in a while. Even though he had never attended college, Texans supported their college teams, as it was a religion or something. Generally, he and some of the other agents went to the sports bar. Today was different. Today, LizzyBeth would be there working, and he hoped to get her to sit down and enjoy the time with him.

Yeah, he was seriously attracted to her, but she kept the professional persona on all the time, even when he flirted. Sure, he had seen her blush a time or two—he secretly loved that—but he wanted to ask her out. He didn't want to lose her altogether, though, and if it meant he had to renovate his home again and again to be around her, he would do just that.

Cowboy double-checked the kitchen and refrigerator. He had plenty of water for LizzyBeth and plenty of beer for him. Not knowing what snacks she liked, he had purchased a variety, more than they could eat in one sitting.

The doorbell rang, and he checked his watch. Excitement

rippled through him. LizzyBeth was early. Great, he would have time to chat with her before she got lost in her work or the game began, whichever she chose. He opened the door with a smile and instantly lost it when he saw who stood on his doorstep.

Ballpark, Doc, Romeo, and Speedy stood there with a case of beer and grins a mile wide. They didn't know anything about LizzyBeth, and he wanted to keep it that way. He had to get rid of them.

Instead, Doc led the way into the house, pushing past Cowboy. "We figured you needed company today. 'Bama is going to put a whoop-ass on A&M, and we'd hate to know you're here crying alone."

The others followed Doc into Cowboy's home—uninvited—laughing. He loved his fellow agents, but today wasn't the day for them to be there. He had to call LizzyBeth and tell her to wait until Sunday to come work on his kitchen. The others would hound him about having a female handyman—no matter how sexy she was. Well, precisely for how sexy she was. What big, bad alpha male hired a woman to fix the sink or toilet? He would never live it down.

He closed the door and walked inside. "Let me make a quick call."

"Oh, did we interrupt something?" Ballpark pointed to all the snacks. "Or were you planning to drown your sorrows in munchies?"

The group of men chuckled. He knew they were not all 'Bama fans, but they partnered up against A&M and him.

Just his luck.

The doorbell rang. Shit. Too late to call LizzyBeth. Cowboy would have to turn her away at the door before the men saw her.

Cowboy opened the door to a smiling LizzyBeth. His stomach fluttered. She looked terrific in her jeans and T-shirt with her raven hair pulled back in a ponytail and no makeup. She had that clean, girl-next-door look that all boys loved.

"Look," he said. Before he could continue, he felt the presence behind him.

"Ooh," said Ballpark. "No wonder you didn't invite us over." Ballpark turned to the others. "He had plans with a woman."

The leather couch creaked when the others stood to see who Ballpark was talking about. Speedy approached, and Cowboy closed his eyes and sighed.

"I'm sorry," he said to her. "My friends dropped in to watch the game. We can reschedule if you'd prefer."

She smiled, and his heart clenched. Beautiful. "No, it's okay. I can work and keep the noise down for the game." She stepped inside and held out her hand to Ballpark. "Hi, I'm Elizabeth, the handyman."

"Dude," Speedy said to Cowboy as he slapped him on the shoulder. "You have a female handyman?"

"That's awesome," Ballpark added. "Come in, Elizabeth. Watch the game with us."

They wanted to grill her, Cowboy could tell, and he didn't want that to happen.

"I was supposed to work today," she told them. "But, if

it's okay with Cowboy, I'll watch a bit. I'm a huge 'Bama fan."

His friends laughed. "Dude," Speedy said, "even she's rooting against you."

"What?" she said, looking at Cowboy. "Oh, I should've guessed. All Texans love A&M. Well, I'm sorry to say they're going to get their butts whooped." She grinned and flicked his cowboy hat brim. "Roll Tide."

He loved her playfulness. This interaction was the first time they'd had this type of camaraderie. "Well, we'll see about that," he said. "Would you like something to drink?" At least she had agreed to watch the game instead of the guys watching her butt while she worked in the kitchen. And they would have.

As he expected, she said, "Just some water."

"No, you have to have a beer with us," Speedy said.

"No, she doesn't," Cowboy countered. "She has what she wants."

The men chuckled at him. What had he done to deserve that? He led LizzyBeth to the kitchen. Before he could make it there, his doorbell rang. Who the hell now? It was supposed to have been only him and LizzyBeth, and now it was the guys and her—too much testosterone in the room.

"I'll get it," Ballpark said. He opened the door. "It's another woman."

The men chuckled and headed to the door like little schoolgirls.

Cowboy looked over and stopped, stunned at who stood on his doorstep. His heart sank, and his gut clenched. It couldn't be. He walked to the door. "Jasmine, what are you doing here?"

Her sweet smile worried him. "Aren't you going to invite me in?"

He wanted to shout "No!" especially with the men and LizzyBeth at his home. How would they respond when they learned he had been keeping this part of his life secret? He couldn't bring himself to speak of his life before the air force and before HIS. However, he knew he couldn't keep her on his doorstep. Instead of stepping outside with her, as he should do, knowing her mouth, he invited her in. Opening the door wider, he said, "I have company, so please behave."

He had to get everyone out of there and find out why this woman, of all women, had showed up on his doorstep. Something had to be wrong for it to happen, and hell must have frozen over or someone was seriously injured or in trouble.

Once inside, he glanced guiltily at LizzyBeth before he introduced his newest guest. "Everyone, this is a friend of mine from back home. Jasmine"—he nodded to the group— "this is everyone." He didn't feel the need to introduce them personally because she wouldn't know them.

"From home?" Danny questioned. "Back in Texas?"

"Yes. I'm Jasmine Vaughn, Michael's wife and the mother of his child. I'm here to bring him home where he belongs."

Aghast, Cowboy stiffened while the guests in the room quieted at the proclamation. He chanced a glance at LizzyBeth and saw the hurt he had never wanted to see etched on her face.

4

COWBOY NOTICED LIZZYBETH couldn't escape fast enough. She grabbed her purse from the kitchen bar and almost jogged to the door. As she slipped past Jasmine, she nodded and smiled. "It's nice to meet you."

Watching her grasp the doorknob, Cowboy desperately said, "LizzyBeth, wait."

She didn't wait. Outside, Cowboy caught her arm, though, and halted her retreat. "Wait, LizzyBeth. Let me explain."

She turned and exuded a stern look filled with distrust. "There's nothing to explain. I'm your handyman, and you're my client. I shouldn't have even been here today except to work."

"I wanted you here today. I like you, LizzyBeth."

"Maybe you should be saying something like that to your wife." She jerked her arm away and ran away from him before he could deny Jasmine's statement.

Anger flashed through his veins. His anger targeted Jasmine for lying her ass off. He turned to the men, and they sat on the couch and chair just staring between him and Jasmine like it was some damn show. "Get out," he told them.

"We never get to witness the good stuff," Speedy said with a fake pout.

Romeo, the quiet one of the group, finally spoke. "I didn't know you were married."

Ballpark just laughed. "This is better than 'Bama beating A&M."

Jasmine. That little bitch. After some ribbing, the men left but made sure to tell Jasmine they enjoyed meeting her.

Cowboy turned to her after closing the door behind his friends. "What are you doing, and why would you lie and say you're my wife?"

"Well, darlin', I once was."

"Was *is* the operative word there. The one you should have led with."

She slunk to him, acting as if she planned to seduce him. He knew her moves and wouldn't fall for them. "Why the fuck would you say you're the mother of my child?"

"Well, that is the truth."

"We don't have a child."

"We once did. Don't you remember our sweet Lauran Belle?"

Oh, he remembered his daughter. He thought of her every single damn day she had been gone. Damn it all. He didn't need Jasmine coming here to remind him he had lost a child. His friends didn't need to know that either, but he would have to explain at some point. They would investigate on their own if he didn't after Jasmine had dropped that bombshell.

"Again, why are you here?"

"It's time you came home. The ranch is falling apart, and your brother has a broken leg from a car accident. He's been drinking instead of supervising the rebuild."

"What rebuild?"

"Oh, that was my idea."

What the fuck was she doing giving ideas to his brother? "Why?" was about all he could get out. Then Cowboy remembered how Jasmine and his brother had betrayed him. He had caught them kissing one evening when he was supposed to be staying out on the range but had come home to see his wife. See her, he had. Unfortunately, it had been in the arms of Nick, his brother.

"Something needed to be done since the last storm almost destroyed the ranch. But things keep going wrong, and your brother doesn't care."

He shook his head. "Why are you involved in our ranch? Don't you have enough to do at yours?" He and Jasmine had grown up together, next-door neighbors—well, neighbors with a few hundred acres in between.

"Franklin has everything going fine at our family ranch without me."

"And why are you involved in my family's ranch?" He was tired of asking questions repeatedly. She was good at diverting his attention to something else.

"Your brother was drunk, and someone got hurt putting a new roof on one of the guesthouses. We didn't know what

22

to do."

"Okay." He realized they were still standing near the door and invited her into the living room to sit. After they sat, he said, "My mom can run things."

"That's just it. No one is running things. Oh, and you have a big balloon note due next month that your brother says he can't pay."

Holy shit. What the fuck had gone on at the Vaughn family's ranch, the Rockin' T? He had left Nick in charge, but his mother could run it if she wanted to do so. She had been beside his father all that time.

It took him back to the days they had all been happy on the ranch. He and Jasmine had been so much in love, and their little daughter had been a sweetheart. His sister, Becca, or as he called her "Sweet Pea," enjoyed the time together with the family. He and Nick jointly ran the ranch, and their mother played the dutiful grandmother. Then Lauran Belle had died, and later Jasmine and Nick betrayed him. So, he had left for the air force, leaving it all to Nick and Becca to manage.

"Okay, since you seem to be in the know, just spill it all."

She smiled proudly. She had won some battle he didn't realize they had played. "Well, there's the balloon note, and the business has suffered because maintenance is required, and your brother isn't paying attention."

"So, are you and my brother an item now?"

"Oh, darlin', I've never stopped loving you."

He held up his hand, palm out. "Stop right there. I don't

want to hear that bullshit."

"It's not bullshit."

Not wanting to hear more, he said, "Tell me about the ranch."

"Okay, I had a brilliant idea to fix up the dude ranch and invite CEOs from companies who offer retreats to their employees. Do the full works like before, with trail rides and roundups but add masseurs and a spa experience. The whole ranch experience plus luxury. If they love it, they'll book their employees."

"Since you seem to know about the money, will it be enough to cover the balloon payment?"

"Oh, darlin', they're coming for free. It's the bookings they'll do that'll cover the balloon payment."

"Let me get this straight. We have a balloon payment"— Cowboy caught he had said "we" and not his brother but continued—"and you suggested we bring in people for free and give them the works?"

She beamed and almost bounced in her seat. "Yes. Brilliant, isn't it? Oh, Michael—"

He cringed at the way she said his name. He had hated it ever since the two had split.

"It'll bring in more business."

Now might not have been the right time to try this marketing tactic. Cowboy saw the logic and agreed it was a good plan, but the money worried him. He needed to find out what was going on at the ranch, but that would mean confronting his brother, something he hadn't done since he walked away and handed it all over. Well, he hadn't legally handed it all over. The ranch still belonged to the three of them—Nick, Becca, and him.

Dare he go home? Maybe he could just speak with his mom and get things straightened out. He spoke with her once a week, and she had yet to say anything about problems.

"You said problems, as in plural. What's going on?"

"Well, there was the employee who fell. Remember Juan?"

Cowboy nodded. He remembered the little man. He had always been eager to join in on anything they did at the ranch, especially horse training. However, he had stopped short of attempting to physically break a horse. Cowboy, Nick, and a couple of other cowboys did that job.

"Then, some of the wood for a guest house went missing." She ticked it off her finger like she had a prepared list. "Then there was the small brush fire."

He sat up straight. Fire on the range could be deadly, and it moved fast, and the cattle and horses were at risk.

"Don't worry," she said. "It was put out fast." She ticked off her second finger. "Then—"

He held up his hand again. "Enough. I'll call Mom and see what's going on. You go home and stay out of our ranch business."

"Oh, darlin', I can't do that. Your sister is counting on me to help her with this retreat."

Damn it all to hell. He would have to go home or have Jasmine run them into the ground. "Fine. I'll go home." That was the last thing he wanted to do, but it appeared he would have no choice.

He only hoped when he returned that he could explain to LizzyBeth because she had come to mean something to him. He wanted to start something fresh with her if she would ever forgive him.

5

MARRIED? CHILD? He said to wait and let him explain, but she couldn't. He would just lie. That was what men did when they got caught in the web of their deceit. With her track record in men, she found that she didn't trust anything that came from their mouths.

She had found herself attracted to Cowboy, which didn't work well in her professional life. He was her client, nothing more. Although it went against her financial needs, she would opt out of remodeling his kitchen and ultimately end their relationship completely. Cut it off now before she believed another lie and fell for someone who cheated on his wife and family. Of all the lies to catch him in, she wouldn't expect him to cheat on his family. He had seemed so normal. Then again, so had Sean Howe.

Elizabeth needed her best friend, the Hallmark Channel, and ice cream—preferably not in that order. Ice cream always came first in times like this. She had been bonding with Cowboy over the time she had worked on his house. She loved that place and all he had been doing to update it.

Even though some of it probably hadn't needed to be done, he had insisted.

She phoned her friend. "Susan, he's married."

"Who's married?"

"Him" was her only qualifier.

"Oh, you mean stud client."

Elizabeth laughed and opened the freezer. Only her friend could come up with a name like that. "Yeah, him."

"I'm on my way. Don't open the ice cream until I get there."

She looked in the freezer and grabbed a pint of Rocky Road ice cream. "Too late." It wasn't, but she needed the ice cream for her broken heart—no, not a broken heart because her heart wasn't yet engaged. Or maybe it was… a little. Okay, it was involved a little too much.

"All right. I'll pick up more and be right there." Susan disconnected the call.

Elizabeth found a large spoon in the silverware drawer and opened the ice cream. Eating straight from the pint, she dug in for a large bite. Once she put it in her mouth, she moaned. Everything would be better with her good friends Ben and Jerry.

She had eaten half a pint before Susan made it to her apartment with two more pints of ice cream—one Chocolate for Susan and another Rocky Road for Elizabeth.

After Susan settled in beside Elizabeth with her ice cream, she waved her spoon at Elizabeth. "Spill." She took a bite. "This shit is amazing."

Elizabeth didn't see the thrill in plain chocolate, but she

kept her mouth shut on the topic. "He's married, and he has a kid."

"Are you sure?"

"His wife showed up and introduced herself."

Susan's face fell. "Oh no. That had to be horrible."

"Worse. Cowboy's friends were there and didn't say a thing."

"Assholes."

Susan had a different vocabulary than Elizabeth. Elizabeth tried not to curse. Oh, she wasn't perfect, and an "Oh shit" would pop out from time to time, especially if her hammer mistook her thumb for the nail.

"I'm with you, sister." Elizabeth dug the spoon into her ice cream cup only to realize she had already eaten the entire pint. Great, now she would have to run extra miles to burn off the calories. Men were not worth the trouble, except for babies, and they were great at giving a woman babies.

"Were any of them cute?"

"Any of who?" Elizabeth asked, confused since they'd been discussing Cowboy.

"The men he works with," Susan clarified.

Elizabeth couldn't believe her friend had already turned them from assholes to cute. But Susan did have a one-track mind. In the gutter mostly.

"Sure. Cowboy's friends are all good-looking men."

"Hmm. Maybe it's not a total loss and you could hook up with one of them."

Elizabeth tossed her spoon at her friend. "I wasn't hooking up with Cowboy. I was working for him."

Susan rolled her eyes. "Sure, honey. No man needs that much work done to his place, and they're handy themselves. Besides, I thought you said you got sexual vibes off him."

She had. More than once too. "Well, cheaters do that, now don't they?"

"Did he at least try to explain?"

She scrunched up her face. "Cowboy tried. I wouldn't let him lie to me. I mean, what could he say?"

"That they were getting a divorce or something."

Elizabeth hadn't thought of that.

"Or she was some psycho stalker who lied."

She laughed at Susan's crazy statement. "No, he would've told me she lied."

"But," Susan said, pointing her spoon at Elizabeth again, "you didn't let him explain, did you?" She took a bite of ice cream, then put the top on and set the container on the coffee table. "Are you still going to remodel his kitchen?"

"No way."

"I thought you needed the money to pay off the debt that ex of yours left you with. Do you have anything else lined up?"

She dropped her shoulders in defeat. She needed the work, and because Cowboy kept adding to the workload, she hadn't seen any other clients to bid on new jobs. "No. I'm screwed." She would have to show up on Monday to begin the job. If he still hired her. She covered her face with her hands. "Oh, Susan, how can I face him? I ran out of there so fast." She opened her hands and looked at her friend. "I was a big chicken."

"Cluck, cluck," Susan said, and they fell into a fit of laughter, like little schoolgirls.

Once they caught their breath, Susan said, "At least it can't get worse."

"What if she's in charge now that she showed up at his house? I'd die of embarrassment repeatedly." Not to mention, she would like to rip every hair out of the beautiful Hispanic woman's head.

"Well, let's work on finding you new gigs so you can offload him and his wife."

"That's a great plan." After her ex, she hadn't thought she would ever like another man again, but she had started to like Cowboy.

He had been charming and the perfect gentlemen around her. She loved him in his cowboy hat and boots, and he appeared as such an authentic Texan. The allure drew her, and his wonderful personality and flirting made her want him like no other man before. It sucked that he was married and had a kid. She could only hope they were divorcing or something, because she wasn't sure she could drop her desire for him that quickly.

6

COWBOY HADN'T BEEN home in nearly fourteen years. He missed his mother, but she had visited him wherever he landed, most recently in Baltimore. He planned to remain there for as long as HIS allowed him to blow shit up.

His mom—Deidra—had turned fifty-five on her most recent birthday. On her last visit, she had brought his kid sister, Becca. He still couldn't believe the little tyke was twenty-eight. In his mind, she was still his little Sweet Pea. He looked forward to seeing them both.

On the other hand, he needed to tear his brother a new one. Not only had he ruined Cowboy's marriage—well, that wasn't entirely true, Cowboy and Jasmine had already had problems after the death of Lauran Belle—but now his brother was supposedly running the business into the ground, if Jasmine hadn't lied.

After he had kicked Jasmine out of his home in Baltimore, he had called his mother, only to find out she had no idea what was going on at the ranch. She had complete faith in her eldest son. His sister, on the other hand, had given Cowboy an earful.

Yeah, he was going to kick his brother's ass from here to Sunday.

After landing at San Antonio International Airport, he rented an SUV for the hour drive home. Home. He did miss the place, the cowboys, the roundups, and all the fun. Heck, he even missed busting broncs. He winced, his body remembering that activity.

He tensed as he turned off the highway onto the dirt road leading to the ranch entrance. What would he find?

"He's running the place into the ground," Jasmine had said. "Things go wrong, and he doesn't care."

Well, Cowboy would soon find out the truth. He drove through the gates of the Rockin' T Ranch and smiled. He was home—albeit for a bad reason, but he was home. If only he could visit without his brother to handle.

Once he had exited his SUV, his sister ran from the front yard into his arms, almost knocking him down. "Sweet Pea," he said. After picking her up and spinning her around, he set her down. "Let me look at you." He stepped back, looked her up and down, and smiled. "How are you still single? I'm sure I'll be fighting off the men for you."

Becca blushed and playfully swatted at his shoulder. "Oh, you. It's about time you got here."

His mother saved him from a rebuttal, coming up for a hug. "Mom, I missed you."

She pulled out of his arms. "I missed you too. So did this ranch. Becca's been updating me on what's happening. I'm sorry, son. I had no idea Nick wasn't doing anything or why I wasn't told until now."

"It's okay, Mom." He went to the rear of the SUV, opened the back, and retrieved his luggage. "We'll get this place ready for the new grand opening."

Cowboy had wrestled with the idea of strangers on their land, but their parents had been excited about the venture. Before their father had passed, they had transformed the ranch into a dude ranch offering authentic cowboy stays. He missed the man who would have kept the family together, somehow.

They entered the home, and nostalgia hit him full force. He remembered all the times he and his siblings had run through that door to watch their father break a bronc or help their mother gather eggs. They'd loved playing on the ranch.

He dropped his luggage and moved further into the home.

"Oh, look," his brother said from the dining room table. "The prodigal son returns." Nick lifted his glass in a toast toward Cowboy.

Jasmine sat beside him and smiled sweetly. "You made it."

What the heck was she doing at their family dining room table? "Hello, Nick. Jasmine."

He turned to his mom. "Is my room still available?"

"Sure enough, son. It has fresh linens on the bed."

Cowboy spun toward the front door, grabbed his bag, and headed to his old bedroom. After all, he wasn't ready to confront his brother, especially not in front of everyone. Especially not with Jasmine there. Why had she inserted herself into his family? She was his ex.

He looked around his old room. His mom had put his old rodeo trophies on a shelf after he had boxed everything up to toss out when he'd gotten ready to leave for the air force.

"She's my wife now," Nick said from the doorway, a bit of a slur to his words. Good grief, it was only noon, and his brother was already drinking.

"Who? Jasmine?"

His brother crutched his way into the room and dropped on the double bed. "Yeah, Mom pretty much insisted after you left."

Surprised, he wanted to feel sorry for Nick, but he couldn't. He and Jasmine had been fooling around while Cowboy had been married to her, and they deserved each other. If only he hadn't insisted his brother and Jasmine's names were never to be mentioned to him, he wouldn't have been caught off guard about the marriage. Still, why wouldn't someone have at least hinted?

"Good for you, brother."

"I take it Jasmine came after you instead of going shopping in Dallas yesterday."

Cowboy studied his brother. Nick appeared older than thirty-five years old. He had hard lines on his face, and he looked a bit sickly when a cowboy usually had a bronze tan on his face. "What's wrong with you? What the hell has been happening?"

"I suck at this, that's what."

"What do you mean? The ranch ran itself." That was

what his dad had always told them when he spent time with them, because he wouldn't be that father who worked all the time and didn't spend time with his family.

"We had a bad two seasons with low attendance. Then the last few storms had done significant damage to the buildings. It's just taken more and more money, and I had no idea of the balloon note."

"Tell me about it."

"Apparently, Dad had been so sure about the success of becoming a dude ranch that he had taken a large loan to build everything with a balloon note fifteen years into the future. Which, by the way, is coming due, and we don't have the cash to pay it. He never expected our troubles and that we'd have a storm destroy most of the buildings before we earned the money."

"Talk to the bank."

"Don't you think I did?" His brother's heated words asked for a fight that Cowboy refused to give him. Sure, they would tumble when growing up, but they were men now, and Cowboy wouldn't fight a temporary cripple, physically or verbally.

"I'll talk to them."

"You're loaded. Why don't you just bail us out?"

He wasn't loaded, especially not to the degree of the balloon note. He had just always been tightfisted with his money until he had met LizzyBeth. Then, he had eagerly dived into his savings for the projects he had had her complete. He missed his time with her, and he hoped when he returned she would give him a chance to explain.

"Take me for a tour. Tell me what's been happening and what's going to happen. I understand we have one week to get ready for the CEOs?" he asked.

"Yep. Good ole Jasmine and her marketing ideas."

Well, at least someone had ideas.

After a ranch tour, Cowboy realized he would have to remain until everything was complete. There had been problems, delays, laziness, and no oversight. In other words, his brother had given up, and they weren't ready for visitors—especially not an elite group that could bring more business to them.

They needed help, though, and he knew exactly who to call. First, he called Boss to let him know he would be gone longer than planned. Then he called Trent McKenzie, the Hamilton half-brother, who owned a ranch in Montana. After that, he had the most important person to ask for help. If only she would take his call.

As expected, LizzyBeth didn't answer the phone. He predicted that but hadn't prepared anything to say on a message, so he stumbled through it. "LizzyBeth, she's not my wife. I need your help. Please call me back."

There. That should cover everything—everything I should have said before she ran off.

Would she fly out and help? They needed someone skilled in multiple trades, like a handyman. The cowboys were trying their best, but they were hired to ride, rope, and entertain, not build or fix anything more than fences.

He needed LizzyBeth. Unfortunately, he needed her in more ways than one.

7

ELIZABETH LISTENED TO Cowboy's message for the third time. "Not my wife." She kept pausing after that statement. Why had he not just said that to begin with at his house? Why allow the woman to lie in front of her and his friends?

"I need your help." What kind of help could he need? Did he still want her to update his kitchen? Now that she knew he wasn't married, she could do it. Her heart yearned for the times they had spent while she worked. She worked, and he would leave her alone at first; then he talked and joked and flirted like crazy. It had always made the days and evenings go fast.

After listening to the message one more time, she called her friend, uncertain of how to handle the situation. "Do you think I should call Cowboy back?" she asked Susan.

"Yes. Let him explain. Besides, it sounds intriguing to just ask for help. That's different than I need you to work, don't you think?"

"Okay, I'll call." Cowboy's message sounded

interesting, but she had to get up the nerve to make the call.

After hours of procrastinating, she phoned him. Cowboy answered on the first ring.

"LizzyBeth," he said. "I'm glad you called back."

"Why wouldn't I?" *Because I'd been insanely jealous of a gorgeous woman who claimed to be your wife?*

"LizzyBeth, she's not my wife."

Relief soared through her after hearing it from him again. "Oh? Why would she say something like that?"

With a frustrated sigh, Cowboy said, "She's my ex-wife. And we divorced when I was twenty years old."

She raised a curious eyebrow she knew he couldn't see. "And your child?"

"I don't have any children." He took a deep breath and let it out slowly.

She wanted to ask more, but it didn't sound like this was a topic he was ready to discuss. Besides, she had heard him mention his aversion to children many times. If only he knew....

"Listen, I'm home in Banderas, Texas. We have a dude ranch, and it needs your TLC. I'd like to fly you down here and have you work on it this week. That is, if you're still free."

She had had no idea what to expect from his plea for help, but this hadn't been something she would have anticipated. Fly to Texas and work for a week with him. Jealousy hit her hard. Would that other woman be there?

"Um...." She thought hard on it. She had bills to pay and no other jobs lined up, but there was only one hitch.

"I'd need to bring someone with me."

"Sure, we could use the help."

Help, Ethan wouldn't be. She had to tell him the truth but couldn't bring herself to do it. What if he changed his mind? She needed the work, and his kitchen had gotten put on the back burner. "I'll make the travel arrangements."

"Just bill me," he said. Oh, Elizabeth would, for her ticket, not Ethan's.

After about five minutes of discussing the work needed, they disconnected the call. Elizabeth immediately phoned Susan.

"Girl, you didn't tell him you have a kid?"

"Well, no. It never came up."

"You mean just now when you spoke with him. Couldn't you tell him your plus-one is a four-year-old? Didn't you say he had an aversion to kids?"

He had mentioned it more than once, although he did visit his friend Ballpark—another strange name—and helped him babysit the bosses' kids. Maybe doing it for the boss made it an okay thing. Surely, he couldn't hate all children. No matter how macho he tried to act, she had seen his kindheartedness.

"No, I couldn't tell him. I decided I'd just show up and wing it. I really need this gig."

Susan sighed. "Girlfriend, you're going to have some explaining to do."

Laughing, Elizabeth said, "It can't be worse than explaining a suddenly appearing wife." She could laugh now only because, in their call, Cowboy had explained his ex-wife married his brother. Why he had shared that tidbit, she could only guess was in hopes of digging himself out of the hole he had ended up in when Jasmine landed on his doorstep.

"We'll see," Susan said. "Pack sexy." Her friend ended the call.

Pack sexy? She was going to work—nothing else.

Elizabeth looked at her watch. Time to pick up her little man from his grandmother's. Thank goodness her mother was retired and loved watching her grandchild. It allowed Elizabeth the freedom to work evenings for those clients who couldn't be available during the day.

She grabbed her keys and purse and charged out the door. They needed to stop and pick Ethan up a few things for the trip, and he could use some cute cowboy boots if he was going to be on a ranch.

Ethan loved horses. She hoped someone would be there to help keep him entertained, so he wouldn't get in the way of the working cowboys. Like before her mother retired, Elizabeth could watch him while she worked. He was an obedient child. But there might be times she needed to do work where she couldn't protect him. Maybe she could hire a sitter part-time. She would make enough to cover the cost—barely, but she would.

At her mother's, she explained the trip. "It's for a week, I think."

"Do you need me to come and watch him?" her mother asked.

Bless the woman, but she couldn't see showing up with

both. "No, I think that would be too much to ask."

"He can stay here for that time."

Elizabeth had thought of that, but she didn't want to leave her son for that long. Plus, her ex was still arguing about custody. He kept threatening to take her back to court as an unfit mother so he could have full custody instead of shared custody. She didn't need to abandon Ethan for a week.

"No. I need this job, and it'll be good for Ethan to be around the horses."

"Horses!" her son exclaimed from the living room floor where he had been playing.

Her son was excited about the trip—not that he fully understood. She hoped Cowboy wouldn't send her back once he saw who she'd brought with her. They had never discussed her kid. She didn't disclose her personal life with clients unless they asked—even then she didn't say much— and Cowboy had never asked. Thank goodness, since she knew how he felt about kids. But why would Jasmine have said she was the mother of his child? Was she that much of a liar?

Elizabeth didn't look forward to facing Jasmine again, but she guessed if the woman had married Cowboy's brother, she would be on-site. She already knew not to trust her. What else would she pull while Elizabeth was there?

Doggonit, she was jealous. That didn't bode well for her trip.

8

COWBOY'S EXCITEMENT GREW about seeing Elizabeth again. Something about the woman warmed his insides and made him feel like a young, lovesick fool. Oh, he hadn't acted like that around her, but he had felt it deep inside. They were destined for each other. Maybe short-term or perhaps for a long time, he didn't know. He only knew they would be together.

He hadn't asked about the extra person she was bringing. Help was help, but what if that help was some husky man who had her eye? He had never asked if she was dating anyone, and they hadn't gotten that personal. Yet. Oh, he would find out, quick. He planned to use this time to charm her even more than he already had.

Her rented car arrived, and he quickly shot a glance to the passenger seat. Empty. Maybe her help turned her down. That was okay; he had good cowboys who could follow orders, even from a woman.

He slid down the ladder from the roof that they were shingling to greet her. Maybe that move would impress her.

But when he turned, she was looking in the back seat. She must have put her bags there instead of the trunk. No matter, he would have plenty of time to do impressive things for her.

With a halt to his step, Cowboy started. Not since high school had he tried to impress a girl. He was a grown man. That wasn't how you won over a woman. Charm. Manners. Those were things you used. At least, that was what he had used in the past, and he had never had problems getting a woman—except for this one. But he hadn't really tried.

Cowboy had just reached the car when he saw a little boy emerge behind the open car door. A child? Had she brought a child? No. He had no idea she would bring a child here, of all places.

With a swift memory of Lauran Belle, he took an oath not to allow the same thing to happen to this child—to whom he presumed was LizzyBeth's child. Why had he never asked? He couldn't go through the heartache of losing a child again.

That meant he couldn't woo the mother, and it would be wrong unless they had a quick fling and nothing else. Only, he had planned more than that for them, and now, it was all garbage.

How could she not tell him she was bringing a child? His temper climbed. He was furious with her for even thinking it would be safe. Christ, she was going to be working all day. Who did she expect to watch her child? Sure, there were enough women around here who would want to do so, but that was beside the point.

"I'm sorry," she said as she approached. "I plan to hire a sitter from town to watch him, if that's okay?"

No, it wasn't okay, but he did need someone to help get the ranch ready. And he still wanted to be around LizzyBeth. He enjoyed her company, even though they hadn't spent personal time together. Before he could respond, the welcoming committee approached. Thank goodness Jasmine wasn't with them, because he could still wring her neck for her deceit.

"Who is this little cutie?" his mother asked.

"He's adorable," Becca said.

Great. Cowboy couldn't say anything now, could he? "LizzyBeth, this is my mom, Deidra, and my sister, Becca. As for the little man, I think you just found two sitters who will not require payment."

"You bet I'll watch him," Deidra said. His mother looked at him. "Are you all right?" He met her gaze and nodded.

She knew how much it had torn him up to lose his little girl. She also wanted more grandchildren, but he had sworn never to give her another. A child should never die before the parents. Never!

"What's his name?" Becca asked.

The little boy stuck his thumb at his chest and said, "My name is Ethan Silas Howe, and I'm four." He tried to hold up four fingers but fought with hiding his thumb. He eventually used his other hand to hold his thumb down and displayed four fingers. Cute. Lauran Belle had never lived to see four. Would she have been as precious?

LizzyBeth turned to his mother. "My name is Elizabeth, and this"—she put her hand on Ethan's head—"is my son Ethan. We appreciate you inviting us."

"Well, you're going to work for it," Cowboy said.

"I know. But I hope it's okay that I brought Ethan. I just couldn't leave him for the week." She looked as if she wanted to say more but stopped. Curious. Maybe she didn't have the support back in Baltimore to leave him. Where was the father of the child? Was he not involved? He knew they had divorced and she had taken over the business. She had explained that the first time she showed up on his doorstep instead of the expected husband. That had been a pleasant surprise, although he had been suspicious of her accomplishing the work. But she had proven she was an expert in many areas and could outperform many handypersons.

"It's better than okay," his mom said. "We've needed some little ones around here, and I'm going to be too old to play with them if I wait for my kids to provide me any more."

Cowboy cringed. He hoped LizzyBeth missed the "more" part of his mom's statement. He didn't want to speak of his daughter. He glanced in the direction of town where his daughter's grave was. He had visited it yesterday, and while he had fought it, tears had flowed. Now, she would have been a teenager if he hadn't left her at the ranch with only Jasmine.

"You said your name is Elizabeth, but I thought Cowboy said LizzyBeth?" Deidra said as a question.

"For some reason," she confided, "he calls me that."

"Let's get you all settled in," his mother said. "Son, get her luggage. Grab a hand if you need help. Becca and I will get them situated. We only have one room inside, and we expected to put your helper out with our hands in the bunkhouse. Is it okay if Ethan sleeps in the room with you? We have a rollaway bed we can bring in."

Hell's bells. If her son slept with her, Cowboy certainly wouldn't get the opportunity. That hadn't been in his plan. Yet, his plan had changed with the arrival of her son. What was his new strategy? He still wanted to sleep with her, and there was probably nothing she could do to change his need for her.

He grabbed the two suitcases from the trunk. One large and one kid-size with SpongeBob SquarePants on it. A kid. He still couldn't wrap his head around that, and he didn't want a woman with a kid or children in general. Why had he not asked her?

Most women talked nonstop about their children, and LizzyBeth hadn't mentioned hers once. He had to rethink his feelings for her. Could he walk those feelings back just because she had a kid?

9

As it turned out, Ethan was a cute little tyke. He entertained everyone with his antics, and his laughter became contagious, even with Cowboy. He could find himself liking this kid. Ethan reminded him of AJ Hamilton's little boy, Ace, who was full of personality at such a young age and whip-cord smart.

His mother and Becca had taken charge of Ethan's care, leaving LizzyBeth free to work. After the two of them had toured the ranch, she had decided to work on the wiring in the cabins, leaving the hands to finish the roofs. He had known that she was a certified electrician and a plumber, which helped him accept her taking over tasks he would have given to a professional.

What was he saying? She was a professional. LizzyBeth had always been professional. Sure, she had blushed when he flirted with her, but she had never teased back—except to tell him 'Bama would win. He couldn't help but chuckle. *Roll Tide, my ass.*

She approached him outside the main house. "Cabin

One's lights are working. I installed the lights on each side of the beds as you wanted, and I think it's a good touch for those who like to read at night."

That had been Becca's—the reader and dreamer of the family—idea. She had taken several architectural design courses in college and had drawn out the interior of the cabins' updates. His sister had talent.

"I need a hand, though. I can't hold the headboard up and screw it to the wall. Busy?" LizzyBeth asked him.

Not for her. "Nope." He dropped the shingles he had been bringing to the men, leaving them for the hands to grab for themselves. He had a woman to help. The woman.

He almost tripped over his feet. *The woman?* Surely not since she had a child. No, not the woman. Just another woman he desired. He hated lying to himself.

They entered the cabin, and Cowboy looked around. The last time he had been in this cabin, there had been a broken table, no blinds or curtains hung, and no working lights in the bathroom. LizzyBeth had been busy, and she was terrific.

"Okay, let me put my muscles to work," he joked, holding up his arms to show his muscles. His short-sleeve T-shirt slid up his arms, and he didn't blush over it. He wanted to impress her but playfully.

She laughed. "Ooh, big man on campus."

Cowboy touched the tip of his cowboy hat. "You betcha, sweet lady."

He hefted the wooden headboard and held it in place while she attached it to the left side of the wall. Instead of regular headboards on the bed frames, they had decided on this design. He liked that it meant it would be harder for their rowdier guests to break. One never knew what they would get.

The bed frame slipped, and he grabbed it before it could fall on the right side. "Oh shit."

"Language," she said and looked at him with wide eyes. "I'm sorry," she hurriedly said. "I'm so used to correcting people's language around my son. I'm really sorry."

He laughed at her stumbling through an apology. "It's okay, and I do need to clean it up. The boys are always on me when I'm around the HIS children."

"I always find that funny you call them that instead of the family name."

"Well, the Hamiltons are HIS. So, it stands to reason, so are the children."

At this point, Boss and Stone were the only non-Hamilton family agents with children—that he knew of. And Boss's child was an adopted son from someone who tried to kill Boss and Jesse, the big boss, the Old Man. Oh, and Sugar had also been captured. That was a crazy time. But the boy had been blameless in his mother's rampage.

The door opened, and Deidra and Ethan walked into the cabin.

"We came to see Momma," Deidra said.

"Yeah, see Momma," Ethan copied. "Momma, look. I colored this for you." He held out a sheet of paper. "It's a horse."

LizzyBeth looked at Cowboy apologetically and went

to her son and took the sheet. "Ethan, this is a beautiful horse."

"He loves horses," Deidra said to Cowboy.

He got the hint. "Hey, little man, how about I show you some real horses?"

Ethan jumped up and down in his adorable cowboy boots. "Yeah, horses."

Cowboy looked at LizzyBeth, asking for belated permission, and she seemed to understand and nodded. He hadn't thought to consider her before introducing the boy to the horses, and it seemed natural to be the one to show him the herd.

"Let's go." Cowboy grabbed up the boy and, once outside the door, swung him up on his shoulders like he had done with Lauran Belle many times. Only Ethan was a bit larger and heavier since Lauran Belle had never seen her second birthday.

They walked around the yard to the corral where Rick worked a new colt. Perfect. A small horse for a small man. He waved the ranch hand over.

Cowboy turned to LizzyBeth. "LizzyBeth, this is Rick Myers, our ranch foreman. Rick, this is LizzyBeth, the handyman, and her son, Ethan."

Rick tipped his cowboy hat like any real cowboy would do and said, "Howdy. Nice to meet you." He looked up to Ethan and cocked his head to the colt. "Want to pet this little beauty?"

Ethan bounced on Cowboy's shoulders, and Cowboy thought the boy might bounce right off. "Momma, it's a baby horse." Ethan squirmed. "Down." Cowboy helped the kid climb to the ground.

Ethan reached through the fence and tried to hug the horse, but he couldn't get his body through far enough. With one hand, Ethan petted the black colt with glee. He giggled and bounced in place.

LizzyBeth laughed and told Ethan to be careful. She looked at Cowboy and mouthed, "Thank you."

His heart went into overdrive with a need for this woman. Kid or not, he would have her in his bed. Oh, he couldn't keep her since she had a kid, but he would have her before she went back to Baltimore and her life without him.

10

ELIZABETH ENJOYED THE times she spent with Cowboy, even though it meant work. She had never looked forward to a job as much as this one, and she knew it was because of him.

Everyone had welcomed her son, fighting over who would watch him, except for Cowboy. He tended to avoid Ethan, and showing him the horse had been the first time he had shown him attention. Maybe his focus on the ranch kept him from having fun with Ethan. She knew if she wanted something with Cowboy—and she did—Ethan was part of the package.

She couldn't just have a fling with someone. She was a single mother and had responsibilities to her son. In no way would she parade men around and then, once her son got attached, take them away. She played for keeps, which was why she hadn't played.

But with Cowboy, she wanted to play, which was a problem of ginormous proportions. Oh, how she wanted to play, though, but never at the expense of her son.

"Earth to LizzyBeth," Cowboy said.

She came out of her daydreams enough to hear him. She shook her head to clear it of the nonsense. "Yes?" she asked as she looked down at her dinner plate. She had barely eaten a bite, and she was full. The cooking could win awards. Their guests were in for a big surprise if these women cooked for them.

"Do you think we'll be ready for the CEOs?" Cowboy asked, apparently again.

Elizabeth picked up a glass of sweet tea—something she was growing accustomed to—and took a drink before responding. The timeline would be tight, but she could make the opening happen. "Yes." She set her sweating glass down before water dripped from it.

"Aren't you hungry, dear?" Deidra asked.

They had worked hard that day wiring, reworking, and building, and she was tired. Too tired to eat, but she still had a son to worry about. He needed a bath and bedtime story. Thankfully, he had already eaten. The women were trying to fatten him up. Elizabeth didn't like the sound of it, but a little spoiling would be okay.

"I think I'm just tired. The food is magnificent." She pushed her plate forward and dropped her napkin on the table.

Deidra smiled. "Why don't you go take a hot bath and get in bed? We'll get that little tyke taken care of for the night."

"I'll give him his bath in my bathroom," Becca pipped up.

"I'll get him to bed," Deidra said. "Story and all."

Elizabeth could get used to this. She only had her mother to help. "Thank you. I'll take you up on that tonight."

She stood from the table and strode to her guest room. A bath sounded heavenly. Her muscles were a bit sore after all of the lifting she had done that day moving furniture in the guest cabins.

In her en suite, she ran the water as hot as she could stand and added the bubble bath that had mysteriously appeared on the rim of the tub. They had planned this evening, those wily women, and that was okay because she was reaping the benefit.

After slipping down in the deep cast-iron tub, she sighed. Her muscles sent her love for the relief they found in the hot water, and heaven was just one step away from a good hot bubble bath.

She heard the knock on her door and slid down in the bubbles. Feeling silly, she laughed. "I'm not available," she shouted.

Not hearing a response, she closed her eyes and inhaled the lavender scent from the bubble bath. Yep, just one step away.

Her door opened and closed, and she panicked at the steps she heard. Someone had entered her room, but maybe they were putting her son to bed. "Hello?" she asked.

"I'm just here to check on you," a deep, male voice said.

She screeched and checked the bubbles wholly covered her. Thank you to whoever put the bubble bath in her bathroom. She would have hated to be in a regular bath with someone in the room. "What're you doing here? I'm fine. Now go away."

Cowboy didn't come into the bathroom but stayed outside the door in the bedroom. She couldn't see him and hoped he couldn't see her.

"Are you sure?" he asked.

"Yes, I'm sure."

"I could scrub your back."

While that sounded good, the answer had to be no. His mother would be there soon to put her son to sleep. She didn't need Deidre walking in on her son scrubbing her back. "No, thank you. Just leave."

"Okay, I will. Just call, and I'll come back and scrub your back or wash your hair."

She heard her bedroom door close, and she relaxed. The nerve of Cowboy to enter her bedroom. Then she giggled. Had he really thought that would work? At least he respected her enough not to come into the bathroom.

Elizabeth remained in the tub until she turned pruned. Then she toweled off, moisturized, and put on pajamas. When she went into her bedroom, she immediately noticed the rose on her bed.

She had never pegged Cowboy as romantic, and the gesture made her heart pitter-patter for him. It couldn't do it for long because a knock on the door and the noise told her Deidra was there with her son. Time for bed.

She looked at the bedside clock—eight o'clock on the dot. The woman stuck to the schedule she had laid out for her son.

Opening the door, she said, "I'll take it from here, Deidra. Thank you for everything."

After reading to her son about frogs in the ponds, she dozed off herself. Her dreams were full of Cowboy and his washing her back in the tub.

* * * * *

COWBOY TOSSED AND turned. His cock hardened while thinking about LizzyBeth naked in the bath. He had wanted to walk into that bathroom so badly, but he wouldn't without an invitation. He hadn't expected one, but he had to try. It had been time to see if she was as far into having sex as he was, primarily since Ethan had been otherwise occupied.

She wasn't ready. Cowboy expected her uprightness had to do with being a single mother and being in his mother's home. He respected that. However, those reasons didn't play well in his favor. The mountain he had to climb with her got steeper every day.

Around midnight, he decided to get up and have another piece of peach cobbler. It was quiet when he left his bed and slipped downstairs. He hadn't expected to scare someone.

"Cowboy," LizzyBeth said after she had stifled her scream, "you scared me."

"What're you doing down here?" He looked at the cobbler on her plate and knew. "Mom's rule is no dessert if you don't eat your dinner," he teased.

"Yeah, well, that's a rule for her kids, not her guests."

He grabbed the milk from the fridge and snagged a glass from the cupboard. "I think I'll have some of that." He pointed at the cobbler sitting on the table by her plate.

She pushed it his way as he sat across from her.

"Couldn't sleep after all?" he asked.

"I dozed for a bit but woke up hungry, so I decided to see what survived dinner. I hit the jackpot with this cobbler. It's delicious."

He would bet she tasted delicious also. *Get your mind out of the gutter.* "Mom is a fabulous cook, and her desserts are to die for," he said before grabbing a fork and wolfing down a bite straight from the pan.

LizzyBeth gasped. "Cowboy, your mom will have your hide for doing that."

He knew she would, but he dug out another bite. "Mm-hmm."

"Why didn't you tell me your name was Mike or Michael? I've been calling you Cowboy all this time because that's the name you gave me."

He didn't mind Mike so much, but he hated Michael because Jasmine called him that. Everyone at the ranch called him Cowboy or Mike, except his bitch of an ex-wife. When Jasmine called him Michael, it ground on his nerves.

"I go by Cowboy. My family calls me Mike." He shrugged. "I prefer Cowboy."

"Is that your"—she used air quotes—"secret code name?" She giggled.

"Oh, ha, ha, ha. It's just a call sign. All of the guys on

the teams have one." Except for the Hamilton brothers. He wondered why they had never used them. The agents had given Jesse one—Old Man—out of respect for his position as leader, but no one dared provide the brothers with a call sign, even though Matt surely had one from his SEAL days.

She took another bite and moaned. Cowboy's blood ran south, and he shifted in his seat. His sweatpants were not much help in hiding his excitement over being near her.

She had crumbs on her face from the bite. "You have some"—Cowboy pointed to a spot on his face—"here." He about died when she stuck out her tongue and slowly licked the area. He knew she wasn't trying to be sexy, but dammit, she had been.

After she missed the spot, he reached over with his thumb. "Here." He wiped the piece of cobbler from her cheek.

She surprised him by grabbing his hand, putting his thumb in her mouth, and sucking off the dessert. A thrill of anticipation leapt up his spine.

He groaned. "Good God, LizzyBeth, you're killing me." He stood, leaned over, and helped her stand. Pulling her close, he said, "I'm going to do something I've wanted to do since I met you." He leaned in and touched his lips to hers, gently molding their mouths together.

He had wanted this woman in his arms since she had shown up on his doorstep with her toolbox. Now, he had her in his arms and willing. But how ready was she? When she put her arms around his neck, he darted his tongue in her mouth and moaned. A passionate kiss was one thing, but sex was another.

Cowboy rubbed his hand up and down her back, pulling her as close as possible so he could feel her unbound breasts mold against his chest. He explored her mouth with his tongue, eliciting a moan from her. Good God, his cock was hard for her.

Knowing if he didn't stop now he would drag her to his bed all caveman-like, he pulled back from her. Her closed eyes fluttered open, and raw desire pooled in them.

"I think I'd best stop now before I do something you aren't ready for."

She searched his eyes and nodded, confirming his thoughts. Dropping her arms, she stepped back. "I think I should go back to bed."

Against his better judgment, he nodded in agreement. "I'll clean up the mess." He would be part of that mess tonight. "Good night, sweet LizzyBeth."

"Good night, Cowboy."

He watched her walk away in the long pants and short-sleeved shirt of her panda pajamas. Damn, she had a fine ass. He wished he could grab it and haul it up to him. He stopped himself and adjusted his erection. He needed to clean up and take a cold shower.

They may not have made it to sex, but he knew she wanted him as much as he wanted her. Now, to win her over for sex.

11

COWBOY HAD KISSED LizzyBeth, and she hadn't slapped him. She had kissed him back with a similar ferocity and desire. That had to be a plus. So, the question now was how did he get her in his bed without the kid around?

The answer came to him. To win LizzyBeth's favor, he had to befriend the kid also. He didn't know if his heart could take that since this wouldn't be forever. Would he hurt the kid after he walked away? And he would walk away. No ifs, ands, or buts about it. He didn't want to hurt the kid, so maybe he needed to rethink his grand plan in more detail.

Today, he needed to meet with the banker and see what he could work out. He had dressed in clean jeans, a button-down shirt, and his cowboy boots and Stetson—his general look but dressier. Ranchers didn't wear suits to do business. They wore suits to weddings and funerals, and not always was that a given.

Arriving at the bank, he took a moment to steady himself. His brother had explained the note and the banker's unwillingness to work with them. Cowboy had to try to get the loan changed, as Cowboy worried Jasmine's plan—while he had unwillingly admitted was a good one—might fail.

He climbed out of his rented SUV and strode into the bank.

"Hi, Mike," a female voice purred as he entered.

He spun and saw Kelly Lynn Ladner standing behind a teller window. They had gone on two dates in high school and used to make out behind the bleachers. Boy, she had aged well. He headed to her window. "Well, hello, Kelly Lynn. It's damn good to see you. How's life?"

She held up her left hand, displaying the large diamond wedding band set. "I married Lincoln Danvers, and we have three kids."

"Congratulations." Cowboy remembered Lincoln. He had been one of the pencil-neck geeks in school. The word was that he had made it big in Silicon Valley, sold out, and moved back to Banderas. Kelly Lynn had always wanted the finer things, and he guessed she had finally gotten them.

"Are you here to do some banking? I can help," Kelly Lynn said.

Cowboy shook his head. "No, I'm here to see Paul." Paul Gregory, the bank manager, had been two years ahead of Cowboy in school. They had never moved in the same circles in school, but he knew of him since Paul had been class president Paul's last three years in high school.

"Oh," Kelly Lynn's face fell, and she frowned. "He's not in a good mood today."

Just great. That was what Cowboy needed, a grumpy banker when he wanted to negotiate. "I'll have to take my chances, darlin'," he said before turning toward the bank manager's office.

Cowboy knocked on the open door, and Paul looked up. "May I help you?"

"Yeah." Cowboy's gut clenched, and he hated being nervous. "I need to speak with you about our loan."

Paul studied him and then snapped his fingers. "The Rockin' T. You must be the long-lost son, Michael Vaughn."

Out of habit, Cowboy cringed at the use of his full name. "Yeah, that's me."

Paul stood and waved at the chairs in front of him. "Come in and have a seat."

Cowboy stepped into the office and sat. He fidgeted with his jeans before speaking. "I want to discuss the balloon payment and see if there is any way we can move that or refinance?"

"Give me a minute." Paul tapped on the keys on his keyboard and waited. After a minute, he nodded. "Okay, let's see. I remember speaking with your brother, and there was nothing I could do. Let me double-check."

Cowboy shifted. They needed options. Nick hadn't been very forthright about his meeting with the banker. After Cowboy finished up with the bank, he would need to tackle his problems with his brother next. Jasmine, the ranch, his brother—thank goodness he'd come home to fix everything.

"I told your brother, if he made a significant down

payment on the balloon note, I could refinance it again for him to give you a few years. But he said he didn't have the money."

"How much?" Cowboy asked, afraid to learn the answer—damn Nick for not telling him this part of the prior conversation.

Paul quoted a figure. Cowboy nodded absently. He had that much saved, but it would be everything he had. He cursed his brother again for not keeping up with things.

"Why that large of a payment?" Cowboy asked.

"Because of the size of the note," Paul said.

"So, if we can make the partial payment, we can refinance the rest into a normal loan?" Cowboy had to be sure the ranch could make the payment if he scheduled it.

Paul nodded. "Yes."

"By chance," Cowboy said, "exactly whose names are on the loan?" He remembered his old man bringing him to add him to the account, but he couldn't say the same about Nick and Becca. It wasn't something he had considered when he had left in such a rush.

"It's the Rockin' T account, but the personal names on it are only yours and your mother's."

Why had no one told him? How had Nick been doing business? His mom must have been doing the banking, or Kelly Lynn just helped knowing Nick ran the Rockin' T. Well, he'd get this fixed before he left. Nick and Becca would be on the account, and they all would be responsible for it, not just him.

"I appreciate your time," Cowboy said. He stood, and

so did Paul. Holding out his hand, he shook the banker's. "If we can't come up with the balloon payment on time, I'll be here with that down payment. Thank you, Paul."

Paul nodded.

After waving goodbye to Kelly Lynn, Cowboy left the bank but didn't feel lighter. Did he want to use everything he had been saving for his future to salvage the ranch he didn't live at and never would? Then he thought of his mom and Becca. Yes, he would do anything for their future, but dammit, he shouldn't have to do so. His brother should have taken care of this matter long before now.

After he arrived back at the ranch, he sought out his brother. He wanted to smack the man for allowing everything to fall through the cracks. Cowboy found Nick lying on the bed in his bedroom with his broken leg propped up on pillows. It felt wrong to beat a man when he was already down, but Cowboy had had enough.

"How's the leg?" he asked, feeling bad that he didn't care if it hurt.

"It hurts," Nick responded.

Ignoring that, Cowboy tore into his brother. "Why the hell didn't you tell me we had a refinance option?"

Nick scoffed. "So you could come in and save the day and show everyone how much of a loser I am? No way."

"I hate to say it, brother, but it doesn't take me to show people that. If you'd quit drinking and actually run the ranch, no one would think you're a loser."

Nick scooted up on the bed. "Listen to you, Mr. High and Mighty. You got out, remember? I was stuck here and had to marry Jasmine, and she's a bitch."

Cowboy rolled his eyes. "Divorce her then."

"She already said if I did, she'd sue for part of the ranch. I refuse to allow anyone outside the family to have it."

Cowboy wanted to beat some sense into his brother. "Then why did you allow us to get stuck with that balloon note and no savings? Why haven't you been running the ranch?"

"Fuck you, Mike. You just don't get it. If you lived with Jasmine and ran a ranch where everything seemed to go wrong, you'd drink also."

He might, but never in excess like his brother had been drinking. "It's about time you stopped drinking then." He would dry out his brother if it was the last thing he did on this visit. With that statement, he whirled and left the bedroom, intent on clearing out the alcohol in the ranch house. His brother would have to go to the bunkhouse for a drink, and with his leg, he didn't crutch around very well.

Jasmine tried to stop him from pouring the bourbon down the drain. It did bother him to waste alcohol that way, but it was for an excellent reason. Cowboy could survive the week without a drink, and he would figure something out when they stocked for the guests.

Deidra hugged him and smiled after Cowboy drained the beer from the fridge. "I'm glad you're here," she said. He knew that meant she appreciated his attempt to dry out his brother.

It was only a start. A drunk always found alcohol, so Cowboy would keep his eyes open.

With the uncomfortable task out of the way, he needed to see LizzyBeth. Cowboy had some wooing to do. He scoffed at the feminine term. He had to win her over, and he knew one trick all chicks dug. He only hoped he would survive.

12

ELIZABETH WAS RELIEVED Cowboy had been off the ranch that morning. Embarrassment infused her from her willing kiss the previous night. She had acted like a woman in heat, and it wasn't like her to be so free. But she had so wanted that kiss. The problem was she had also wanted more, and she wasn't sure she was ready. Sure, she had convinced herself she was ready, but something had changed. She didn't understand why she held back. Who was she fooling? She knew exactly what was stopping her—Ethan.

Would she never have sex again? Maybe if she hadn't brought her son along, she would feel freer to go to Cowboy's bed. But she had brought him, and things were as they were.

Early afternoon, while working in guest Cabin Five, finishing up trim work, she heard a commotion outside. Worried Ethan may have gotten into trouble, she set down her paintbrush and ventured out to see what the fuss was all about.

To her surprise, the handful of cowboys and extra

workers for cleaning and cooking for the guests surrounded the horse arena, shouting and laughing. One of the hands—Spencer—rode a bucking horse inside the fence. A wild horse. She quickly searched for Ethan to ensure he didn't get into harm's way. Relief surged through her when she saw Cowboy holding the boy on his shoulders. The picture they made melted her heart.

Why did Cowboy say he didn't care for children when he had treated Ethan with such attention? Sure, he had avoided her son initially, but look at them now. Adorable. Maybe this could work. When they returned home, they could be a couple and, eventually, a family. She was getting ahead of herself, because she wasn't ready for another family where men cheated.

A cry came up from the crowd, and she caught Spencer sailing over the horse's head. He hit the ground with a loud thud. After a moment, he jumped up and out of the way of the bucking horse. As he moved, he grabbed his cowboy hat off the ground. These men were never without those hats, except at the dinner table.

Then Cowboy handed Ethan off to Becca, who set the boy on the ground and held his hand. Ethan put his other hand on the fence rail and peeked through the slats to see inside the arena. Cowboy, however, slid through the railings to enter the area. He strutted—yeah, strutted—toward the now resting horse and Spencer, who dusted off his denims.

After a few terse words to Cowboy, Spencer moved away. Her heart nearly stopped. Did Cowboy intend to try to ride that beast? It was a beautiful horse, but it was wild, and she had just seen it throw the ranch hand high above its head.

Sure enough, Cowboy grasped the reins, put his foot in the stirrup, and gracefully swung up into the saddle. Then, all hell broke loose on that horse.

Elizabeth pushed forward to the fence and gripped the railing, ignoring potential splinters, and sent up a quick prayer for Cowboy to be safe. She watched as the horse bucked and turned, doing everything to rid itself of the annoying rider on its back. Juan, standing near her, softly counted the seconds. Was there a time limit to breaking a horse? She had heard of "eight seconds," but she thought that was bull riding.

Meanwhile, Cowboy hollered and whooped his way through a bucking ride on a wild horse. The ride seemed to last forever, and he never let go of the reins with one hand. His other arm was out beside him, balancing him through each buck in the air, as she had seen on television.

He rode until the horse gave up the fight and calmed. The men cheered, and he slid down the side of the horse as if it were a park slide. Spencer—who didn't look like a happy camper—came forward to take the reins to cool the beast down.

Ethan, she suddenly worried. She was going to kill Cowboy for giving her a near heart attack. She had been so focused on Cowboy that she had forgotten her son had been out here and potentially in the way. Elizabeth found Ethan still with Becca, now clapping and bouncing up and down. She smiled at her little man's excitement.

Cowboy came over to her and righted the cowboy hat he had plucked up along the way. "Hey, darlin'."

Heat rose in her face. Then she remembered the fear Cowboy had put in her. She slapped at his shoulder. "Don't ever scare me like that again."

He acted as if the swat had hurt before laughing. "There was no reason to be scared. I've done that my whole life."

"But you're not a real cowboy any longer. You're some super-secret agent who plays with guns now, not horses."

Cowboy cocked his head and raised his eyebrows. "Were you worried about me?"

She could truly slap him for being so obstinate. "Of course I was worried about you, and I also worried when Spencer rode the horse. It's downright dangerous."

Becca arrived beside her.

Ethan shouted, "Mommy, did you see Cowboy ride the horse?"

Elizabeth boasted a big smile for her son, acting as if she wasn't angry at Cowboy. "I saw." She leaned down and picked up Ethan, adjusting him on her hip. He was too big for this, but she couldn't let go yet.

"Can I ride the horse?" Ethan asked.

She glared over her son's head at Cowboy. "No. That horse is dangerous."

Cowboy jumped in. "Tell you what, little tyke, I've got a horse that I think we can ride together that your mom will think is safe."

"Yippee!" Ethan cried out before Elizabeth could stop the conversation.

"I don't know about that," Elizabeth said, frowning over how she would get her son's interest diverted from horses.

"LizzyBeth," Cowboy said, "trust me. I have the perfect mount, and I'll be riding with him."

She narrowed her eyes. Why the sudden interest in her son's happiness after ignoring him the first few days? Was this his ploy to get her into bed? It wouldn't work. Or would it? Doggone her wishy-washiness with him.

Good grief, this man drove her crazy. She couldn't figure him out. "Okay, but only if I'm available to watch."

"How about you ride with us? On your own mount, that is," Cowboy offered. "We can ride tomorrow after lunch, and I'll show you part of the trail ride we give the tourists."

"We're in." Elizabeth would be able to watch Ethan. Only, she hadn't ridden since she was a little girl, and that had only been twice. No matter her worry, she would figure it out. It would be bonding time with both Ethan and Cowboy, but she had to decide if that was a good thing.

Cowboy didn't strike her as a cheater, but neither had Sean. What if she and Ethan got close to him and he broke their hearts as her ex had? Elizabeth didn't think she could stand it again. But she would never know unless she tried. She had to watch how close Ethan came to Cowboy because she wouldn't gamble with her son's heart again.

"Good, I'm off to the house for a few. I'll see you later at the guest Cabin Five to see what you've accomplished." He nodded, then strode away.

Becca, whom Elizabeth had forgotten was there, giggled. "He's going to be so sore later."

Elizabeth studied Cowboy and noticed his walk was a bit stiff. "You think?"

Becca nodded. "I know. He rode that horse for a while, and he's been out of the game for a long time. He's going to need a massage."

Her first thought was to offer, but he might expect it to lead to more. She wanted to see him interact with her son—just the three of them. Then she would decide about sleeping with him. Mind made up, she promised herself she wouldn't change it again.

13

COWBOY HAD FORGOTTEN about this part of breaking horses. He remembered the fear and awe in LizzyBeth's face, but he forgot that he would ache all over for the effort. Even his teeth hurt. What he wouldn't give for a massage, especially one from LizzyBeth.

Jasmine walked up to him as he neared the house. "Need a massage? I can give you one, like in the old days." She smiled, and his insides tightened into a sickly knot.

"No, thanks." How could he have ever loved this woman? High school fascination, that was all it must have been. "Don't you remember you're married to my brother?"

"We both know it's you I've always loved," she purred.

He hated when she did that purr thing. Cowboy turned to see his brother standing in the doorway, leaning on his crutches. *Oh shit.* Had he heard her?

"Jasmine," Nick said firmly, "isn't it time for you to help mother start on dinner?"

"Of course, darlin'." She smiled sweetly, and she didn't seem abashed for saying what she had in front of her husband. What kind of marriage did those two have?

"Nick…." Cowboy was unsure what to say to his brother, as he hadn't asked Jasmine for a damn thing.

Nick crutched closer. "Don't sweat it. You did nothing wrong, Mike. I did, and I've let her run free too long."

Cowboy searched his brother's face, seeing the hurt all over his features. Good grief, his brother loved that crazy woman. *Good luck on that one.*

"Do you want me to call one of the traveling masseuses to come give you a rubdown? We have several who come out regularly for the hands. Jasmine hired one to start when the CEOs arrive, and she would probably come out early."

That would go over well with LizzyBeth, he was sure. "No, thanks. I'll survive." He dusted his pants off once more and strode past his brother into the house. A hot bath would do the trick—for now anyhow.

Entering his room, he quickly closed the door then ripped off his shirt and stretched. He felt the pull and bruising. Boy, his muscles hurt. He hoped he had succeeded at impressing LizzyBeth, because his body couldn't take that ride again.

Someone knocked on his door. Irritated it might be Jasmine again, he swung it open. "What?" he growled.

LizzyBeth's eyes widened at his naked chest or his tone of voice. He couldn't be sure, but he would go with her being impressed with his chest, which was better for his ego.

She reached out a hand with a jar in it. "Your brother said you needed this to rub into your muscles, or you'll be sore."

Was his brother trying to undermine him with LizzyBeth by telling her he would be sore? That son of a bitch.

"He also said"—she cleared her throat—"that it would be better if someone rubbed it on for you and to get a good massage deep in the muscles."

Cowboy remained quiet. She was working up to something, and he hoped it was her giving him the massage and not offering to call a masseuse.

"So," she said, "since everyone else is busy, I volunteered." She looked at him and beamed as if she had accomplished something fantastic and was proud of herself.

Yes! "Well, he's right. And, if you're offering, I'll take it." He suddenly realized his best bet would be to be honest about his sore muscles if he wanted her to feel she needed to rub him all over. "I'm already a little sore, and it's been a while." He sheepishly smiled.

She laughed. "But you looked like you did it all the time."

He laughed also. "I used to, but not now. Come on in." He waved her into his bedroom. "I really appreciate your doing this. I was wondering how I'd get my back muscles."

"Well," she said, "I guess you'd best take off your boots and jeans and get on the bed." She looked at him with those big eyes again. "You do have underwear on, don't you?"

He couldn't believe she had asked that. Yet, he had to think. Yes, he did. "I'm good. Turn around, and I'll get ready and under the covers on the bed."

With her back to him, he began to undress, willing his slowly growing erection to heel. It wouldn't do to let her see that right off the bat. Once down to his underwear, he pulled the covers back on the bed, tossed them, and crawled under the top sheet. He lay on his stomach and covered only his midsection. "I'm ready."

LizzyBeth hesitated beside him. Was she scared to touch him? He did have a couple of scars on his back that might repulse her or remind her his work was dangerous.

Cowboy turned his head toward her and watched LizzyBeth open the jar. Were her hands shaking? He didn't know if that was good or bad.

She dipped her fingers in the ointment, which smelled godawful, and tentatively touched his shoulder.

"It's okay," he said. "You can't hurt me more that I already am." That wasn't entirely true, but he doubted she would do a deep tissue massage.

That seemed to relax her. LizzyBeth rubbed in the ointment, gently massaging his muscles. "This stuff smells terrible."

He laughed. "It does, but it does wonders on achy muscles."

"Why did you ride that horse?"

Cowboy shifted and looked up at her. "To impress you. Did it work?"

She smiled, placed her hand on his shoulder, and pushed him back down. "Maybe."

He smiled. *Yes!* It had.

Her touch was magical. She used just enough pressure for Cowboy's muscles to feel the relief pulsing through them, and it was also just enough for his cock to twitch.

"What happened here?" She touched a spot on his back.

"A guy knifed me in the back in a bar fight."

"When did that happen?"

"When I was in the air force." They had all been drunk, and the guy was talking shit about Air Force Special Forces. He and his teammates didn't take the smack talk, and they had all been written up later but praised for standing up for their squadron.

"I didn't know you'd been in the air force. I mean, I've seen some air force items in your home but wasn't sure if it had been you or your dad."

"No, me." He would tell her he had been a PJ, a pararescueman, but that wouldn't mean a thing to her, so he just kept it simple.

She rubbed his lower back, and he moaned. The muscles felt as if they were tearing out of his skin. He had most definitely overdone it with the horse-breaking stunt.

Laughing at his sound effects, she pointed to another spot on his back. "And this one?"

"I was shot rescuing a kid with HIS." He vividly remembered how one of the tangos had slipped behind them and shot him as he climbed aboard the helo. Since it had been such a long shot, it hadn't been bad, but it had put him down for a couple of months. He had hated sitting on his ass while the other agents went on missions.

She moved the cover under his thigh to rub it, and he wanted to moan again. Holding tight to that bronc had about worn out his thigh muscles.

"You're so tight," she said.

And hard, he wanted to add but knew better. He would never be able to turn over if he didn't do something to bring down his erection, and there was no way he could hide it. He tried to recall football stats, but all he could think about was her hands on his cock.

"How long has it been since you've been home?" she asked as she moved to his calves.

"Fourteen years," he said matter-of-factly. And he wouldn't have come home now if he hadn't had to do so. Seeing his brother and Jasmine together was like a knife in his gut because their betrayal had been more than he could bear.

"What happened?" she asked.

He waited a minute, then decided to tell her. "I caught my brother and Jasmine together in an embrace."

She froze her movement at his admission. Then, as if noticing she had stopped, she started back again, working her way up to his calves back to his thighs.

If only she would massage his butt muscles. They needed her hands and the ointment badly. "Oh, is right. Anyhow, it wasn't long after that I joined the air force and took off."

"What about your mom and sister? Don't you miss them?" she asked as she worked the tight muscles, sending ripples of relaxation through them.

"I do, but I see them a couple of times a year when one or both visit me wherever I'm living at the time. They were in Baltimore not long ago."

"Has it been hard coming home?" She paused. "To

them, I mean."

"No. I stopped loving Jasmine a long time ago." Now, why had he said the "L" word about another woman? Idiot. "We were high school sweethearts, and I don't think our love was ever real anyway." There, that should clear up his mistake. It also set his heart free on Jasmine betraying him. His brother, on the other hand....

"Hmph." She skimmed over his butt and went back to his lower back.

"What's going on with your ex?" he asked to turn the tables. "You two used to own the business together."

She stopped for a moment, then continued. "Nothing. Sean gave me the broken-down business in the divorce. He wants back in, but I won't let him."

Her husband wanted back in the business. Just the company or their life also? Cowboy wanted to know but wouldn't ask because he wasn't sure he'd like the answer. "You're doing an amazing job."

She laughed. "With your ranch or the massage?"

"Both." He chuckled. "Now, if only you'll help out my sore butt muscles." *It's worth a try.*

She stopped her massage.

"It's okay if you don't want to," he said. "I can take care of them later."

"No," she said. "I'll do them." She stopped adjusting the sheet. "I'll have to pull your underwear down."

He didn't mind that at all. LizzyBeth's hands on his ass would be heavenly, even if it were to rub his sore muscles. "It's okay. I'll stay like this, so it'll only be my backside."

Sliding his underwear down, she breathed heavily. "Thank you for inviting me this week. And for not being upset about Ethan coming. This trip, even though it's work, has been good for both of us."

She touched his buttocks, and his cock hardened more. He needed to shift to a comfortable position but worried she would get offended if he moved. She wasn't ready to jump into bed with him, although this would be a perfect time. They were alone, and someone was watching her son for her. He would bet his brother had set it up as an apology for Jasmine.

Her hands gripped his buttocks and massaged the lotion into them, kneading as she went. He moaned at the pleasure of her touch and the deep tissue massage. With her help, he might be able to sit later tonight without pain.

After she finished rubbing his butt, she said, "Okay, turn over."

He froze. "Uh, I don't think that's a good idea."

"Why? Have I not done this right?" She sounded worried, and he had to soothe her feelings.

"No, it's that you've done it too well."

It took her a moment, then she laughed. "Okay, Mr. Macho Man. I've got a little boy, and I understand and can ignore certain things. Turn over, and I'll get the front of your legs, then we'll be done."

So, he did. The sheet was tented, and while LizzyBeth stared at it a moment, she did what she said. She massaged his legs. When her hands on his thighs neared his balls, he thought he might come right then and there.

"That's enough," he called and pulled the sheet over the rest of his body. He couldn't handle it anymore unless LizzyBeth was lying next to him.

She smiled. "Yes, it is." Then she winked. "For today." She turned and walked out of the room.

Well, damn. The little minx knew what she had been doing, and she had teased a little afternoon delight. Boy, oh, boy, was he going to have fun with this woman.

14

THE BOSS SAT back and pondered the dilemma. He needed money and that land, not all of it, but the back few hundred acres which were worth a small fortune.

He had ordered sabotage, but the cowboy he'd hired had done little that halted the progress of the reopening plan. He spoke with the cowboy. "Mike has returned, and they might make that payment after all. Which means I'll never get the property."

"It's possible," the cowboy drawled. "He's got everything organized, and with that handywoman, things are moving fast."

"I want that property before they realize it's rich with oil deposits," the boss said. He had secretly done prospecting on Mike's land because so much was untouched and he'd had an inkling it would produce liquid gold.

"They'll never realize that because they'll never check. The Vaughns are not into riches, just that damn dude ranch." The cowboy took off his cowboy hat and slapped it against his jeans before returning it to his head. "And family," he added.

"Then they have to fail in this grand reopening."

"I'm trying, but they keep a good watch on things," the cowboy said. The boss didn't think he tried hard enough, but that was for another time.

"It's time to crank up the problems," the boss demanded.

"Will do," the cowboy said with a smile.

The boss knew he could count on the man to sabotage the projects at the Rockin' T.

But would he do enough? It was time to bring in the big guns.

15

OUT IN THE yard, Cowboy watched Rick and Franklin, their neighbor and Jasmine's brother, ride in at a hard gallop. Their hurried gait suggested something had happened, and Cowboy only hoped there were no injuries.

The two cowboys stopped in front of him, dust rising from where the hooves had churned it up on their halt. "Boss," Rick said, although Cowboy didn't care to be called that, "someone has killed three of our cattle and left the meat."

Cowboy's gullet rose. Killed their cattle? "Are you certain?" Maybe the cattle had died of disease, which could be wrong also.

"Yeah," Franklin said. "They're over near the border between our properties, and my hands saw them over the fence this morning. You might want to come check."

Like he had to be told twice. "Give me a minute to get a mount."

He hurried to the barn, calling Jorge, Randy, and Spencer to accompany him. The four mounted and took off at a gallop, following Rick and Franklin.

His heart crashed. Why would someone kill their cattle and not take the meat? People had been known to kill cattle when they were hungry, but they took the meat. It bothered him that people would steal, but he would rather they didn't go hungry either. Had they come to the door, his mother would have shared everything on her table and in her deep freezer.

The Rockin' T consisted of eight hundred acres that bordered Franklin's twelve hundred acres. The five of them—Franklin, Nick, Cowboy, Jasmine, and Becca—had grown up together and would each travel about a twenty or so minute walk on horseback to visit the other ranch. Becca had always been the odd girl out since Franklin and Nick were in the same grade, and so were Cowboy and Jasmine. Becca didn't like to be left behind, though. If this ride hadn't had a dire reason, he would have smiled at his little Sweet Pea's persistence over the years.

Eventually they arrived at the slaughter. It was just as Rick had said. Three dead cattle and the meat left.

"Rick, find a cell signal and call the sheriff." There was no cell signal in the middle of their range, out in the middle of nowhere. Maybe they should see about a company adding a cell tower to their property, which would help the ranch communicate and bring in extra revenue.

Cowboy continued, "This is not accidental." No way was it. Someone had snuck up on the cattle and sliced the three steers' throats. *Son of a bitch!*

Rick peeled off and trotted back toward the ranch,

giving his horse a rest from galloping since there was no rush.

"It's too late to butcher them for meat." They had been dead too long to recover any beef safely. They would have to dig a large ditch and dump the cattle to keep the wolves at bay. Thank goodness for heavy equipment.

"Boys," Cowboy said to his ranch hands, "you know what to do. After that, do a ride of the entire range for other possible killings." Riding the range meant getting off horseback and onto four-wheelers to cover it in a reasonable time. Still, they had plenty of land to protect.

Jorge, Randy, and Spencer nodded and turned toward the ranch and the equipment necessary to do the job. While it was true men loved their toys, no cowboy liked dead cattle.

Cowboy turned to Franklin. "Thanks for notifying us. Why don't you come to the house? I'm sure Jasmine will be glad to see you. It's time for lunch, and I'm also sure Mom's put on a spread."

Franklin smiled. "I'd love to see her and your family, and I miss your mom's cooking." He rubbed his belly in a hungry gesture.

The two men rode side by side back to the ranch slower than they had set out to check the cattle. The horses needed the rest, and they were in no hurry.

"Jasmine told me about the balloon payment and your problems," Franklin said.

"Did she now?" Damn bigmouthed woman. His brother should have divorced her long ago. Yet, the idiot loved her, so Cowboy was stuck with her in the family.

"She also said the ranch had two offers to buy it out."

"And?" That was news to Cowboy. Neither Nick nor Jasmine mentioned that.

"Well," Franklin said uncomfortably, "I told Nick this, but he said no. If it comes to someone buying it, I'd like to offer to buy it so it can remain in our families. With Jasmine as your sister-in-law, I'd will it to her and Nick."

Cowboy turned and stared at his neighbor. "Really?" That was a considerable expense.

"Well, instead of giving her half of our ranch. I'd rather see you keep the ranch, but I don't want it going to some company who's going to break it up and build some godawful businesses or condos this close to my ranch. I like my peace and quiet."

"Deal." That made sense to him, and Cowboy would do the same for Franklin. He had no other choice, now did he? But he did. He could float the new down payment and refinance the thing. Then, Becca and his mother would have a place for life.

They rode in silence the remainder of the way and headed to the house upon arrival.

Jasmine squealed when she saw her brother and threw herself in his arms as Sweet Pea had done to Cowboy when he had arrived. Women. Cowboy shook his head.

"Mom," he said as he entered the ranch house, "got room for one more at the table?"

His mother peeked outside. "Always for Franklin."

Ethan ran up to him. "Can we ride a horse, Mr. Cowboy?"

Cowboy couldn't get the "Mr. Cowboy" down his gullet, but his mom had been teaching the boy Southern manners.

"After lunch," he promised the boy. He would take him out to see the colt again. The two could enjoy playing in the arena, and maybe they would exhaust each other. "Where's your momma?"

Ethan pointed out the door. "Working."

That didn't help him any. He expected that much. "Thanks, partner." He ruffled the boy's hair and went to search out LizzyBeth.

Outside in the fresh air, his mind whirled as to who would do something so heinous as kill his cattle. What could be the reason? All these little things had to be something more significant. Maybe one of the buyers wanted the property worse than expected. He would have to speak with Nick about the offers. Some businesses would do anything to get hold of prime land like theirs.

Cowboy heard singing from Cabin Five and smiled. LizzyBeth had a good voice, nothing to garner a contract for but enough to make him smile broader.

He walked into Cabin Five to find her wiping down the walls. "What're you doing?" He could see, but it made no sense.

She jumped. "Oh! Why do you keep sneaking up on me?"

He laughed. "I didn't sneak. You were just in your own world. Why are you wiping down those walls? I thought you finished this cabin yesterday?"

"Well," she said and set down the towel on the kitchen

counter, "somehow the walls got dirty and needed touch-up painting and wiping down."

Somehow? What the hell was going on in his place? "How bad?"

"Not really bad," she said. "Some mischief. It's been happening all over."

"What?"

"Haven't the boys told you of missing stuff?"

They had. He had to do something to protect them before something went seriously wrong. He knew who to call for that help. Trent had offered to come, but he wouldn't be enough. The boys would have to put on their cowboy boots and hats and join in the hunt of whoever was trying to ruin the Rockin' T Ranch.

16

SINCE THE ROCKIN' T Ranch had plenty of saddle horses and saddles, Trent flew in the next day with the boys from Baltimore—Doc, Ballpark, Speedy, and Romeo—an hour behind. Thankfully, half of the Alpha and Bravo teams were on break while the other half trained the newly formed Charlie team, so Cowboy had a small group to protect his family ranch.

The men had rented two SUVs, with Doc and Ballpark riding with Trent while Speedy and Romeo rode together. Cowboy smiled at that. Sometimes team assignments were hard to break.

"It's good to see you again," Trent said as they greeted each other in the yard.

Cowboy shook his hand. "I'm damn glad you could make it." Trent managed a ranch and could help Cowboy understand where they had gone wrong and how to fix it. True, Trent didn't run a dude ranch, but he understood livestock and ranch hands and ranch expenses.

The other men were there to help him figure out what

the hell was happening and who was trying to sabotage them. Because, by God, something was happening to make the grand reopening more work than it should be.

Each of the men shook hands as Cowboy welcomed them. He noted Speedy and Romeo looking sideways at the horses in the corral. They had been newer hires that hadn't spent a week a year on Les White's—*God rest his soul*—family's ranch with the others. So, they probably couldn't ride or ride well. Cowboy mentally shook his head. This adventure might be fun after all.

"Y'all will sleep in the bunkhouse," he told them as they toted their bags in that direction. "Lunch is in an hour, and you can eat at the ranch house because Mom is putting on a spread of fried chicken and fixins."

"Oh yeah," Speedy said. The man was in for an awakening. As a Popeye's fanatic, Speedy was about to find out his mother's chicken tasted ten times better.

"Just out of curiosity," Cowboy said, "who knows how to ride a horse?"

Trent adjusted his cowboy hat and nodded unnecessarily. Doc and Ballpark raised their hands. As expected, the two from Bravo team had no experience.

"Okay," Cowboy said, "this afternoon, you two"—he pointed at Romeo and Speedy—"get lessons. The others can watch and laugh their asses off if they like. We plan tonight."

They split, and the men went inside the bunkhouse, and Cowboy returned to the ranch house where the women were busy in the kitchen, even LizzyBeth. He wondered how she and Jasmine were getting along.

The atmosphere in the kitchen seemed light, with no fighting or side glances. That soothed Cowboy's soul. If he had to be stuck with Jasmine in the family, he wanted to ensure she wasn't trying to tear it apart. Her making passes at him was already too much to bear.

"Did they arrive okay?" Deidra asked.

"They're here." He reached for a piece of chicken and got his hand slapped by his mother.

"You'll wait with the rest," she said.

He laughed and stepped out of the kitchen to see Ethan playing on the floor in the living room with plastic horses. The boy was obsessed. Boy howdy, he had been adorable chasing around the colt the other day. Cowboy would have to do that again with him.

"Hey there, little man," he said as he sat on the floor next to the kid. "Whatcha got there?"

"Horses," Ethan said without looking up. He galloped a horse to a plastic corral and put it away, only to grab another horse and do the same. "It's time for lunch, and they need to eat," he said.

"Did you name them?" Cowboy had consistently named his horses when he was a kid. He remembered the year he numbered them and his father said he should use more imagination. So, he had named his horses Corral, Barn, Bunkhouse, and Ranch. His father hadn't been impressed.

Ethan pointed to a black one. "Buck." He pointed at a brown one with spots. "Spot." He pointed at another. "Frog." Then pointed at the final one. "Steve."

Cowboy wondered at the naming but remembered the boy was only four and he had his own way of figuring names.

Deidra leaned in the living room. "Ring the dinner bell, son."

Cowboy leaped to his feet and went outside to ring the large bell that signaled all sorts of things but right now meant lunch. After the bell, everyone should stop work and enjoy lunch unless they were on the range.

The cowhands ate in the bunkhouse, and the men took turns cooking, or Deidra sent food over. Today they would also have fried chicken, mashed potatoes and gravy, homemade macaroni and cheese, buttered corn on the cob, and Becca's amazing biscuits. For dessert, they had banana pudding and apple pie.

Trent and the agents made their way inside, and he introduced them to the women. The men seemed a bit nervous about meeting Jasmine since Cowboy hadn't explained the situation yet, so he had best do that later. Otherwise, the men would speculate and start rumors. Yes, the men of HIS gossiped like little schoolgirls.

After Deidra asked Cowboy to say a prayer—something he hadn't done in a long time—they dug into the meal. The serving platters were empty within minutes, the plates piled high with good home-cooked food.

To entertain and embarrass Cowboy, the agents took turns telling funny stories of Cowboy's experiences at HIS, including his most recent death within seconds. He would make them all pay when the right time came.

Later, after the men picked mounts and gave them a test ride, they met in the building used for visitors when it rained to feed them inside or host events. The men sat in chairs in a circle, Speedy and Romeo sitting gingerly after their lessons.

"What's going on?" Doc asked.

Trent had been the only one he had explained everything to, and now he took the time to update the men on all the incidents that had occurred before and after he'd arrived home, tying them all together.

"I fear someone is trying to run us off the land by ruining our grand reopening so we can't pay the note. We've had offers to buy the property, so maybe one of them is to blame."

"So, let's find out about the buyers," Ballpark said.

"My thoughts exactly," Cowboy said. "Since Bravo team is less experienced in riding, they can take the lead on investigating the potential buyers. The others need to help me watch the range. I'm worried this could escalate. Killing cattle is serious and dangerous business."

"You got rifles for us?" Trent asked. "Those could come in handy on the range."

They would if someone tried to sabotage them again. "Sure." They had employed more hands at one time and did during roundup time, so they kept an extra stash of weapons, saddles, horses, and bunks for those purposes.

"What do you think they'll try next?" Romeo asked.

"I don't know," Cowboy said. "And that worries me."

"What's going on with the women?" Doc asked.

Cowboy knew precisely what he meant. "Jasmine is my ex-wife. She's now married to my brother."

"And Elizabeth?" Ballpark asked with his eyebrows raised.

"She's, well, she's LizzyBeth." *The woman* he wanted to say but left off. There was still that little tyke in her life, and he couldn't bear the loss of another child, so that was why she could never be *the* woman for good.

17

Elizabeth knew they would finish the projects in time, so she didn't feel guilty sitting on the quilt outside with her son. Deidra and Becca had set up a picnic lunch for them in the yard under an enormous oak tree. Elizabeth needed a rest. Her mind had been a whirl since she had been in Texas. Being around Cowboy all the time was more challenging than Elizabeth had thought. Harder only in that it ate at her resolve bit by bit until she worried that she would give in and her resolve would all be over.

Ethan finished his sandwich and asked to play, so she cut him free but kept an eye on him. He knew he couldn't go near the horse pens without an adult, but a four-year-old didn't consistently process rules when their desire reigned strong.

"You look relaxed," Cowboy said as he approached. "May I sit?"

She shaded her eyes as she looked up at him. Dang, he was handsome. The cowboy hat did it for her. "Sure." Something was different, and he appeared on edge.

SHEILA KELL

It was when he moved that she noticed the difference and stiffened. He had a sidearm on his belt, and she pointed to it. "Is there a need?" It worried her. She had thought his friends were coming to help finish early, but maybe not. Something was afoot.

He squatted instead of sitting on the ground across from her. "Maybe. Maybe not. I'd rather be safe than sorry."

"Did you find out who killed your cattle?"

He shook his head. "Not yet. Where's Ethan?"

Elizabeth smiled and pointed at her son in the side yard about twenty yards away. Cowboy shifted his body so he could see them both.

"He needs to be careful out there. Snakes."

Her smile faltered. "Is that why we were issued snakebite kits when I got here? Is it that bad?"

Cowboy's jaw clenched, but he didn't answer directly. "Better safe than sorry," he repeated.

"So, you're a safety-first kind of guy?" Her thoughts went to condoms, and she felt heat rise to her cheeks.

He laughed. "Honey, I have a dangerous job, and safety is paramount."

"That's right." She laughed and looked away.

He furrowed a brow at her. "What?"

Her smile brightened as she looked at him. "I was just thinking I should call you Captain America."

"Don't," he said and frowned. "I like to blow things up. I'm sure Captain America would have problems with that."

So, he couldn't take a good joke, or at least Elizabeth thought it a good joke. "I'll call you Captain America anyhow. There are too many cowboys here."

"You could call me Mike," he said, "like the family does."

"Mike." She tried it out on her tongue. "I like it. What about Michael?"

He stiffened. "Never call me that."

Rejection hit her. She had just been joking again, and Cowboy had taken it seriously. What did he have against the name? Jasmine called him that—*Jasmine called him that*. No wonder he didn't like it. Elizabeth wasn't the sharpest knife in the drawer, but she was smart and caught on quickly.

"Okay, Mike or Cowboy it is."

He grinned at her with that sexy mouth. "You can call me just about anything if you put your hands on me again. I feel the need for another massage," he joked.

"I bet you do." She laughed, glad he had let his guard down. "You men are alike. Let the woman do all the work."

"Oh, darlin', I never let the woman do all the work." He winked.

The heat rose to her face again, and her insides did a flip-flop. "You're a hopeless flirt." She liked it, though.

"Only with you, darlin'."

Elizabeth rolled her eyes. There went the lying that most men did. "I'd best get up. It's getting deep here."

They both laughed, then silence seized their conversation. Elizabeth and Cowboy looked at one another, and she imagined the hunger she felt echoed in his gaze.

She recalled his firm muscles and the way she had teased him during his massage. It had been wrong of her, knowing she probably wouldn't—where did "probably" come into it? She would not. No, if she were honest with herself, she would. Just *when* was the question.

Was he a "hit it and quit it" kind of guy? She worried she would be a conquest, so she kept changing her mind. She wanted him, and oh, how she wanted him. But Ethan was part of her equation, and "hit it and quit it" guys didn't make the cut.

"Did you want to go for a ride later?" Cowboy asked. "Ethan has already asked."

She hadn't taken a ride since she had been at the ranch and was second-guessing her earlier agreement to ride. She would probably fall off the horse and break her neck. "No, I'll pass," she said.

"Maybe next time," he said like she would be back at the ranch.

That stopped her for a moment. Did Cowboy plan to bring her back? Maybe he had more work for her. That would be grand but would make things awkward between them one day, or so she suspected.

Suddenly Cowboy jumped up. "Ethan," he said firmly, "don't move."

Her spine straightened as it did anytime someone told her child what to do. Then she heard the noise—a rattle. *Oh, God, a rattlesnake.*

"Mike," she whispered as she helplessly watched her son stare wide-eyed at Cowboy and his command. Her heart clenched, and her stomach revolted. Adrenaline surged through her, but she froze in place. She had to help her son, but was she fast enough to grab him?

Before she could take a step toward Ethan, Cowboy pulled his gun, aimed the distance between them and her son, and fired. He raced over to Ethan, grabbed him up, and ran back to her. Fright laced Cowboy's face. What did he have to be frightened of? It was her son that a venomous snake could have killed. Sure, they had snakebite kits, but they were a long way from a medical facility.

Her heart thudding, she took her son in her arms and squeezed him tight. Tears pooled in her eyes, and she closed them to stave them back. She could have lost her son, and how could she have allowed him to play where there might be danger?

When she opened her eyes, it seemed everyone on the ranch had arrived. The men were all armed and looking around seriously. Heck, even Becca had a shotgun in her arms.

"What?" Romeo asked with his hand on his sidearm.

"Rattler," Cowboy said, keeping his eyes on her and Ethan. Compassion had replaced the fear in his features. "Over there." He pointed but didn't avert his gaze.

Jorge and Rick went over to where the snake was and whistled. She thanked them for not commenting on the size. She couldn't handle knowing how much worse it could have been. If Cowboy hadn't been there….

She swallowed hard. "Thank you," she croaked.

Cowboy nodded, turned, and walked away. He never looked back as he entered the barn with his men following.

Elizabeth turned to Deidra and Becca, who looked at

the barn with concern and then to Jasmine, who had tears running down her face.

"What did I miss?" Elizabeth asked. Everyone seemed to understand what had happened but her. Ethan had been the one at risk, but the ranch acted as if someone had died.

Jasmine turned to her. "Michael and I lost our daughter to a rattler."

18

Cowboy's gut clenched, and he struggled with his emotions. Thank God he had been there to save the kid. If only he had been there to save Lauran Belle. If only….

The ranch hands knew the story and didn't speak. The agents looked at him questioningly. He had never discussed his past life or the fact he had once had a wife or a daughter.

"My daughter—" His voice broke. "My daughter died from a snakebite. I was on the range, and Lauran Belle had been playing in the yard. Jasmine wasn't armed, nor did she have a snakebite kit." He had started handing those kits out when he returned to the ranch. He couldn't believe they only had a few and hadn't given each person one. Snakes were everywhere on a range, and they had to react swiftly to the venomous ones since they were so far from medical care. He refused to lose another person due to a snakebite.

"She didn't have a vehicle because Mom and Becca had taken the only working truck to town for groceries," Cowboy finished.

"Holy hell," Trent said, having kids of his own. Cowboy

imagined he had thought of one of his children and their ranch. "I see why you gave us the snakebite kit, and I'm going to hand them out at my ranch."

Trent didn't participate much in ops as part of the HIS ownership since he had a ranch to run. Learning of his parentage late in life had changed the man, and falling in love had finalized the change. Trent lived in Montana on a horse ranch, which grew larger year after year. Cowboy missed the man at the ops center each day. When there had been only one team of agents, Trent had been their team lead. While he loved Boss's style, he did miss Trent's laid-back stance.

"It's a good idea," Doc said. The medic among them had appreciated the small medical kit he had received. "Although, a Glock is better."

The agents nodded in agreement. Cowboy wouldn't argue there because they believed in alleviating the threat before it became deadly, and that stand was their business as agents of Hamilton Investigation and Security.

"We should fan out and check the yard for more snakes," Romeo said. "It'll be safer for all, especially the guests due to arrive in a couple days."

Cowboy nodded, knowing that was the right course. He had to speak with LizzyBeth and confirm that Ethan was all right. "Go ahead," he told them. "I've got something to do first."

The men nodded and dispersed.

Cowboy took a moment to steady himself. His hands shook, and his insides knotted. If he had missed, the snake would have bitten Ethan. Relief swamped him that his shot had been accurate. The endless days on the shooting range at HIS headquarters had paid off in the right way.

He took a shaky step toward the house. *Please let that boy be okay.* He had seen the boy crying in his mom's arms, probably more scared than anything else. Cowboy knew he had frightened the kid by shouting, then the shot and the way Cowboy grabbed him up so quickly, but Cowboy had had no other choice.

After entering his family home, he stopped. He couldn't believe the sight before him. LizzyBeth hugged Jasmine, and they both cried. Someone must have told LizzyBeth the story of Lauran Belle. Damn. He wanted to be the one to tell her, and he guessed he shouldn't have waited so long.

Cowboy cleared his throat loud enough for all to hear. The women broke apart as if they had been illicit lovers caught in an embrace. He guessed that meant they were not BFFs or anything now. Good. He didn't want Jasmine in his life like he wanted LizzyBeth in it.

He stopped short. What was he thinking? No. Only in his life for a short time. *There, that's better.* "Is Ethan okay?" he asked.

LizzyBeth wiped the tears from her face with her hands. "He is." She rushed to him and thrust herself into his arms, almost knocking him down. "Thank you," she whispered.

Damn if he hadn't wanted her in his arms, but not for this reason. The only reason for her to be in his arms was for lovemaking, but he would take what he could get at this point. Everyone watched, so he gingerly put his arms around her and hugged her back as if awkward and not correct.

"Shh," he told her as he felt her tears on his cheek. "It's okay, and he's all right."

She sobbed harder.

Well, hell. Cowboy looked frantically for his mom as she would know what to do, because he was at a loss. Crying women were not his thing.

His mom had tears silently running down her face also. Hell, all the women were crying. Good grief. The boy had survived. Then he looked at Jasmine. Oh, they remembered his daughter, who hadn't survived. He closed his eyes to the thought. Cowboy had loved that little beauty and her laughter. He missed her just as much today as the day she died.

LizzyBeth pulled back and kissed him quickly on the lips. "Thank you," she said in a normal voice. "Ethan is fine because of you."

Cowboy didn't want to let her go, but she had pulled away, so he dropped his arms. They felt empty suddenly. He wanted to grab her back and hug her for all it was worth.

He cleared his throat again, this time at an average level. "It's okay, and I'm glad I was there."

She turned and launched herself into Cowboy's arms again. "I'm sorry about your daughter." Once again, he felt the tears slide down her face.

Well, hell. Cowboy just might cry himself, and macho men—as she had called him—didn't do that, especially Captain America. If the reason for their hug hadn't been so dire, he might have smiled at that name. He didn't deserve it.

This time, he pulled back. He had mourned his daughter for years, and he didn't need someone else grieving her for him or Jasmine. "It's okay." He set her apart from him and walked around her to the front door. It wasn't okay, but he wouldn't allow her to see that. In his world, men didn't cry, or if they did, no one was to see. It was stupid, but he followed some unwritten caveman rule.

Outside, he jumped in the rental and headed to town. He needed to see his little girl's grave. Cowboy wiped away the first tear that slid down his cheek.

19

ELIZABETH SHUDDERED WHEN the men found a small snake family near where her son had been playing. She was also glad Cowboy hadn't been there to see the nest. No matter what he said, she knew he was upset about the rattlesnake. Mostly, she believed, because he hadn't been able to do save his daughter from one.

She couldn't imagine losing Ethan. It must have been horrible for Jasmine and Cowboy to lose their daughter so young. Her heart went out to them.

Trent approached her, silent like Cowboy. *It must be something they learn at that HIS place.*

"I have a three-year-old and a one-year-old. I'd hate to lose either to a snakebite or anything really," Trent said. "Your boy is okay, though."

Elizabeth's was, and Cowboy's girl was not. "Yeah, I was fortunate." She turned to him from the corral post she had been leaning against, watching the horse training. "Thank you for clearing out the rest of them." Yet Ethan wouldn't be playing anywhere near that area again.

Trent tilted his cowboy hat and smiled with dimples showing on his cheeks. "It was a pleasure."

They turned back to the corral, watching Jorge work a horse. She couldn't understand half of what he said as it was in Spanish. That must mean the others spoke some Spanish if the horses responded to the language. She guessed it must help if someone attempted to steal the horse or Jorge only worked that way.

"You know," Trent began, "Cowboy is a tough nut to crack. We had no idea he had an ex-wife and child. He's a secretive bastard."

Elizabeth had to agree there. Of course, she had never asked personal questions, and Cowboy had never offered information. Nor had he asked many questions of her. Cowboy had had no idea she had a child. She still winced at his initial reaction to seeing Ethan when she had arrived, and now she understood his reluctance to have his own children—no, she did not. She would always want more children.

"Well, we're just handyman and client, so he doesn't owe me his life history," she said, even though she felt differently. Since that massage and, especially, the kiss, they were more. They hadn't said anything nor had more happened, but she felt the difference. Their bodies acknowledged each other when they were close. She craved his hugs as they were insanely erotic.

"Hmph."

Elizabeth turned to him for a second, noticed the slight smile on his face, and turned back to the horse. Maybe they hadn't fooled anyone.

"I'm going to see what trouble Speedy and Romeo are getting into. Bravo team always spells trouble. Enjoy the show."

Elizabeth didn't move as Trent silently walked away. When a car drove down the road leading to the ranch house, she turned. Her heart thumped wildly at Cowboy's return, and she was giddy like a schoolgirl.

Not caring how it looked, she rushed to greet him at the car. When he exited, she bolted into his arms. They held each other with neither speaking. It was a parent-to-parent hug—one of thanks and one of regret.

When she pulled back, he kept his arms loosely around her.

"Well, hello, darlin'," Cowboy said, back to his old self.

She smiled brightly. "Well, hello, you." Yes, she was flirting outlandishly, and she didn't care if anyone saw. It wasn't like they didn't know. Trent's grin had given that secret away, and she might as well enjoy it while she could.

"I just might have to leave again to get this warm welcome," he said with a sexy grin.

Elizabeth pulled completely from his arms. "Ha ha."

Cowboy closed the car door and put an arm behind her back, leading her to the main house. "What's been happening in my absence? Have the boys behaved?"

She wondered about Romeo and Speedy since Trent needed to check on those two but decided it was best not to include that part. "All has been well."

"Good." He nodded. "I picked up some salmon steaks

to toss on the grill tonight, as I thought you might like something besides beef."

Inside, she rejoiced at his thoughtfulness. "That would be wonderful," she said as she patted her empty belly. She had missed lunch worrying about Cowboy and his swift escape. Deidra had suggested he had headed to town and Lauran Belle's grave. That was what Elizabeth would have done had it been her. Thank God it was not.

"Do you speak Spanish?" she asked out of the blue, thinking of the horse training.

"Somewhat, honey. Jorge is one hell of a horse trainer but refuses to teach them in English." He laughed. "He's got us by the—" He halted. "Never mind."

She had an inkling he meant to say "balls" but left it.

After they entered the house, he dropped his arm from her back, and she wanted to reach out and pull it back, but they were around the family. Maybe he didn't want to show them he wanted to be with her. She hoped he didn't plan to keep her secret. Then again, would it be better for Ethan not to know?

Maybe Cowboy was thinking of her boy's heart, which melted hers.

"Mike," Deidra said, "what do you have there?"

Cowboy lifted a grocery bag she had missed. "Salmon steaks. What do you think of grilled plank salmon?"

"My mouth is watering," his mother answered.

Cowboy handed the bag over to Deidra and turned to Elizabeth. "LizzyBeth, let's go check out the cabins and make a punch list. I want to make sure everything that was completed remained so."

That was an odd statement to make. Had Cowboy expected her to lie about her work? Then again, she'd had to repaint part of one cabin. "Okay," Elizabeth said more cheerfully than she felt. At least she would be alone with him. Maybe he would kiss her again, and perhaps she would kiss him. Elizabeth wasn't usually that forward, but she had to take the chances she had since she and Ethan would leave in a couple days.

They exited the ranch house and headed to the first cabin. No one spoke on the short hike, and he didn't touch her. She wondered what was on his mind that kept him from noticing she existed.

When they reached the first cabin, he stopped and turned to her. "I'm sorry."

Confused, she searched his eyes. "What for?" *Please don't let him apologize for kissing me.*

"I shouldn't have run off like I did when you'd had such a fright."

Oh, that. Elizabeth could forgive him now that she knew the reason. "It's okay. You had your reasons."

"I went to my daughter's grave."

Just as Cowboy's mother had thought. Deidra may not see her son often, but she knew him. Elizabeth nodded but remained silent. He appeared to have something to say.

"I couldn't save her," he said, his voice hoarse and raspy. "I was on the range, and I hadn't left Jasmine a working vehicle."

She had learned all of this already, so she remained quiet.

"It was my fault my daughter died."

Oh no. Elizabeth's heart bled for this man. She could see how he would think that, but it wasn't valid. "It wasn't your fault," she told him in vain. "Bad things happen to the innocent, and we don't know why." She wanted to say they had to trust there was a reason but didn't think he would accept that or was religious. Heck, she probably wouldn't have accepted it had she lost Ethan. For them, though, not only had Cowboy been there armed, but he had also handed out the snakebite kits, and there was always at least one extra vehicle on site.

"That's what I hear," he said. "It doesn't change that I lost a daughter."

"No, it doesn't." She reached out and pulled him into her arms, hugging him tightly. Now was the time for her to comfort, not worry about a kiss. That put their relationship at a different level that she wasn't sure he wanted, but he accepted the hug anyway.

20

COWBOY HAD ENOUGH of being alone with LizzyBeth and not touching her. In the fourth cabin, he stopped their progress. No sabotage, so Cowboy felt they might be in the clear. The other incidents had been someone pranking them in the wrong way. With his colleagues on-site, nothing had happened, except *the snake*.

He turned to LizzyBeth. "I'm not going to beat around the bush. I want you in my bed." He touched the bed in the cabin. "In fact, this one will do."

LizzyBeth blushed crimson. Dang, that was cute as all get-out. He watched her eyes flare with passion and knew he had won. "Ethan," she said.

Shit. Cowboy didn't want to hurt the kid, but he couldn't be more to LizzyBeth than a bedmate. Maybe they could hang out, but that was it. While Ethan was a cute cuss, he was a child that could die of a million things before he reached maturity. Cowboy's heart couldn't take another loss like that.

"Ethan doesn't need to know," he said. "I'm not talking

about a lifetime here, and you need to know that up front."

"This is hard for me," she said. "Being a single mother, I have to worry about my son, and I can't just have flings."

Well, hell. Cowboy had thought he had won her over. The massage. The kiss.

"But," she said to his heart's delight, "I want a fling with you."

Hot damn! He stepped close to her and reached out to stroke her cheek with his thumb. "You're beautiful."

LizzyBeth shook her head. "I don't need flattery. I need you."

Things didn't get much more straightforward than that. "Well, okay then."

After removing his hat, Cowboy threaded his fingers through the hair at the nape of her neck, nice and slow. Then he pulled her toward him. *Savage seduction.*

"I'm going to kiss you," he told her unnecessarily.

"Quit talking and do it," she whispered breathlessly.

Leaning down and pulling her up, his lips touched hers, lightly at first. A tentative touch, as if testing the waters. Then, with scorching heat, he pressed hard on her lips and smothered them in a savage kiss. When she opened her mouth to his, he slid his tongue into her mouth, reaching deep to touch her soul. He wanted so much from this woman.

As the kiss deepened, he pulled her tightly against him. He loved the feel of her breasts on his chest. He skimmed his free hand down her back, then rested on her behind— good God, what a sweet ass she had.

He could already tell once wouldn't be enough with this

woman. He might lock them in this cabin until the guests arrived so that he could get enough. Maybe not even then....

Pulling LizzyBeth closer still, Cowboy loved the slight moan that escaped her once she felt him hardening against her lower stomach. He had been working up to wood with the want of her ever since they had been alone.

"You're a great kisser," he murmured against her lips.

"Mmm. So are you," LizzyBeth whispered.

LizzyBeth and Cowboy's eyes locked, and without words, she leaned back. He reached down and pulled her T-shirt off to expose a lacy, pink bra. His mouth watered at the need to taste this woman everywhere. "You're so lovely."

"Flatterer." She laughed and tried to cover herself.

"No." He grasped her hands and pulled them away from her breasts. Breaking eye contact, he leaned down and took a lace-covered nipple in his mouth. His teeth skimmed over her pert bud. "Perfect."

LizzyBeth moaned, and her head lolled back with her eyes closed. *She's beautiful. How did I get so lucky?*

He reached around and unhooked her bra with ease, bringing it down over her shoulders to expose rosy nipples. "Perfect," he repeated, thinking he needed a thesaurus or he would keep repeating the word. Then he leaned down and suckled on one breast while his hand massaged and toyed with the bud on the other.

Again, she moaned, and the sound went straight through him to his rigid cock. He had to have this woman, and now. But he refused to rush things since he might not get another chance with her.

Cowboy pulled back and yanked his shirt over his head. He had to be skin to skin with her—chest to breasts. When the contact happened, he thought he might come in his pants. It felt so right to be close to this woman, which scared him a bit, but not enough to stop loving on her.

He moved them to the bed and knelt one knee on it, then laid them down, her beneath him. Holding himself up with his elbows, he looked deep into her desire-laced eyes. "I want you, LizzyBeth. I have since the moment I saw you on my doorstep with your toolbox. I mean to have you, here and now."

"But the others?" she questioned with a quick shot of fear in her eyes.

He swiftly hoisted himself off the bed, moved to the door, and locked it. Then he returned to the bed, hovering above LizzyBeth.

"No one will bother us," he said. "They've all got work to do, and none of it involves the two of us."

That seemed to appease her because she put her arms around his neck and pulled him down for a kiss. Not just a quick kiss, but a tongue-down-your-throat, I-am-going-to-fuck-your-brains-out kiss. He loved it. If he wasn't careful, he could fall for this woman.

This moment was right—he had his woman in a bed with no one around, and she was already half naked. Then, the moment wasn't so right.

Someone beat on the door, and they jumped. LizzyBeth quickly covered her breasts with her hands as her mouth formed an "O."

He cursed and jumped off the bed, reaching for her T-shirt. "Just a minute," he yelled.

"Hurry, Cowboy," Ballpark said. "Doc's been shot."

"What the fuck?" Cowboy sputtered.

LizzyBeth grabbed her bra and T-shirt and raced to the bathroom while he threw on his T-shirt. He had no idea if it was even on correctly, and he didn't care. He had an emergency on his ranch.

He unlocked and threw open the door. "What the hell is going on?"

Ballpark, out of breath, said, "Someone shot at us on the north range. Doc was hit in the leg. So was his horse."

Of all people to be hit—Doc. He was the one who healed them. Cowboy only hoped he wasn't hurt too much to help himself until they could get him to the hospital. Or he hoped it wasn't bad enough they needed a medivac.

"How is he? Tell me everything." He left the cabin without even checking behind him on LizzyBeth. He doubted she would emerge from the bathroom until they had all left anyhow—what a way to end their monster make out session.

"We were riding the north range," Ballpark said, "when out of the blue, someone began firing at us. We were out in the open and couldn't pin down the shooter, so we hauled tail out of there. In our retreat, Doc was hit in the back of the right leg and his horse in the right flank. Everyone else is fine."

Thank goodness for that sliver of luck. "How bad is Doc?"

"Enough that we're taking him to the hospital. The bullet is still in his leg."

"And the horse?"

"He's still walking around," Ballpark said.

Cowboy spotted Speedy, Trent, and Romeo loading Doc into the back of one of the rented SUVs. "I'll drive," he said.

"We hoped you would since we don't know where to go," Ballpark added.

"Ballpark, come with me." He reached the SUV. "Trent, you're in charge. Mom has the number to the vet, and he'll come out and take care of the horse." He turned to the other men. "Speedy, Romeo, stay with Trent and protect my family. No one goes near the north range until I return."

Son of a bitch. Who the hell would shoot at his men? And why? He was tired of this bullshit, and he would find answers when he returned.

"Hang on, Doc. I'll get you there in a hot minute."

Doc smiled through his pain. "I wasn't worried. Just don't let them take my leg."

Was his wound that bad? Cowboy hadn't looked at it himself. With the SUV in reverse, he pressed the accelerator and raced backward, gravel spinning everywhere. His adrenaline spiked when Doc moaned in the back. He would get his friend to the hospital and ensure they saved the leg.

When he returned to the ranch, there would be hell to pay for someone wounding his friend. He hoped LizzyBeth would forgive him for walking out on her and not looking back. He had some apologizing to do, but the safety of the ranch came first. The term "bros before hoes" came to his mind, but LizzyBeth wasn't a ho, not even close. She was in his heart, and he didn't know what to do about that. He needed to blow something up.

21

THE BOSS WAS pissed at the cowhand in front of him. "I told you to keep them off the north range."

The cowboy shrugged nonchalantly, and the boss wanted to grab him by the shirtfront and punch him in the face. "I can't help what his friends do, and they've taken over as if they're security or something."

"I thought they were there to help finish the building?" the boss asked.

"I think that was just an excuse." The cowboy pulled the toothpick from his mouth. "I hit one of them."

They should have all died. Scaring the men away from that area would only make Mike want to know why someone shot at his friends, and they would be back. This time it couldn't be scare tactics, and it had to be for real—deadly real.

The boss hated it, but they needed that land. "Clear out of the north range."

"Already in the works," the cowboy said.

He was unsure whether to praise the cowboy for acting

on his own or beat the living shit out of him for not waiting for a command. This man, the boss thought, was getting too big for his britches. Something would have to be done.

"Is the ranch ready for those visitors?" He would worry about the cowboy after he owned the land.

The cowboy nodded. "Just about."

"I told you to sabotage their work," the boss said.

"I can't with those men watching over everything like we're criminals or something," the cowboy grumbled.

"Get them to reroute the trail ride away from the north range."

"I imagine that'll happen anyhow, but I'll suggest it."

The boss slammed his fist on the desk. "Dammit! Do more than suggest it, and no one goes near that range right now."

"You know Mike will want to see where his friend got shot."

He did. They would clear out for a day or two and hope Mike didn't realize what they had been doing on Rockin' T land. He had to have that land, and if it didn't go back to the bank, he would never get it. If only Mike hadn't come back. He had to be out of the picture—one way or another.

"Find a way to take care of Mike and his friends where it looks like an accident. I don't mean shooting either." He had to be firm with this cowboy.

"They're not working on the ranch, and Mike only comes out to see what the girl has done. They've got something going on, and they try to hide it, but everyone knows."

Then he would get rid of that woman. No, he wouldn't kill her, but he would think of something.

"Keep them off the north range," the boss said in dismissal, "or you'll be the one to pay."

22

Cowboy decided on skeet shooting since he couldn't legally blow things up at the ranch. The local law authority tended to have problems with someone making bombs, so he avoided that kind of trouble. But he would blow the hell out of a piece of clay.

The skeet shooting had been another of Jasmine's ideas to add to the ranch experience. He hadn't thought it an "authentic cowboy experience," but now he was glad she had purchased the setup.

"Pull," he yelled to Ballpark. With the shotgun, he followed the disc's trajectory, moved forward, imagined he was blowing up the person who had shot his friend, and squeezed the trigger. The clay exploded in tons of fragments. His temper eased only slightly. He had to find out who had shot at the men.

He and the other agents had walked the scene and hadn't found any shell casings, so they could only guess where the shooter had staged himself. It pissed him off to no end.

"Pull," he yelled, angry all over again. With an easy

squeeze of the trigger, he shattered the disc. Once more, he said, "Pull." Once more, he destroyed the clay disc. Yeah, their guests would enjoy this addition.

He needed LizzyBeth. He needed everything about her. His heart beat wildly for her and what they had almost done in the cabin earlier. Had it been only that day? The day had seemed entirely too long.

He handed the shotgun over to Ballpark and decided to find his woman as twilight set in for the night.

There he went again with *his woman*. Had he lost his damn mind? Well, he had to admit he wanted to keep her, at least for a while. And feeling that way before they had sex meant something, and he feared what it was.

Inside the ranch house, he sought out LizzyBeth only to find she had retired to her room with Ethan, who wasn't feeling well. A tummy ache, his mom had said, and nothing serious, thank goodness.

"What do you think?" Trent caught his attention as he was about to knock on LizzyBeth's door. Best he didn't knock anyhow, not with a sick kid. His libido would wait, but it didn't want to wait, yet it could.

"About what?" He had been caught off guard and was unsure what Trent had asked him.

"Come on," Trent said, leading him away from LizzyBeth's door and to his brother's office, which, thankfully, was empty. Once the door closed, Trent continued, "About the shooting and the other problems. What do you think?"

Oh, that. "Someone doesn't want us to succeed. But,

dammit, we will." They were too damn close to finishing, and the guests would arrive in two days.

Trent smiled. "I know you'll succeed, but what are we going to do about the problems?"

Cowboy dropped into a chair. "I don't know. It's like they know what we're doing and are picking small battles, not completely to stop us but enough to hamper our efforts to get out of this hole our dad dug." The balloon note loomed closer and closer. His mother had no doubt they would make the payment, but he wasn't so sure.

"You've got a traitor in your midst," Trent said.

Cowboy stiffened and sat straighter. "Who?"

"I don't know," Trent said before adding, "yet."

Trent was right, and someone had to know what they were doing and what would stop the work. "The shooting, though."

"Spencer was unaccounted for at the time."

Cowboy looked hard at Trent. He had never really liked Spencer, but for him to shoot at the agents? He had a hard time with that one. "I'd like to think one of my family's men didn't shoot Doc or the horse."

"He may not have, and he could have been out on the range elsewhere. I haven't spoken with him yet because he didn't ride in until a bit ago."

"I'll do it." Could one of his brother's men have turned against them? Why? Money would be the only reason, but they paid their hands better than most ranches.

"Not alone," Trent said.

Cowboy appreciated the support because he would

probably kill the man if Spencer were the shooter. "Let's go."

The two left the ranch house for the bunkhouse. There, they found Spencer just getting out of the shower. Cowboy didn't care that the man was half naked; he wanted answers now.

"Where were you this afternoon?" he asked Spencer, who stood with a towel around his waist and one slung over his shoulder.

"The south range," he said. "I wanted to ensure no one had tried to butcher the cows there."

"You know there's a rule that no cowboy rides alone on this ranch," Cowboy said, wondering why he hadn't already throttled the man for disobeying the rules.

"You've got everyone busy doing manual labor," Spencer spat out. "We're cowboys, not roof layers."

While that was true, Cowboy wouldn't take it from this particular hand. "Still, the rule is the rule. Why did you ride out alone?"

"Because no one wanted to go. The hands are focused on getting the work done as quickly as possible, and they didn't feel it necessary."

"Yet, you did?" Trent asked calmly.

Spencer turned to Trent. "Yes," he bit out. "Someone killed our cattle. I'm beyond pissed we haven't done anything about it, and I wanted to make sure no one had done anything to the other cattle."

"But we rode the ranges yesterday, checking for just that," Cowboy said. This asshole needed a laying down, and

Cowboy wanted to be the one to land the first punch.

"We need to check every day." The man was right, but Cowboy wouldn't agree during this conversation.

Spencer looked between the two men. "What's this about?"

"Someone shot one of my men and his horse," Cowboy said with vigor.

"What?" Spencer appeared genuinely shocked. "You think I did that?"

"I didn't say that," Cowboy said. "I noticed you were absent during that time."

Spencer bowed his shoulders. "I didn't shoot your man, and I'd never shoot a horse."

Cowboy didn't know whether to believe him or not. He didn't know Spencer well enough, as he had been hired after Cowboy had left the ranch. "All right. We're sorry to bother your shower time."

Cowboy and Trent turned and left the bunkhouse. It wasn't until they nestled back in the office that they spoke.

Trent asked, "Believe him?"

Cowboy shook his head. "I don't know, and I don't like him flouting the rules and riding alone. That's suspicious, but I can't say he shot at the men because of it."

Trent nodded. "I agree. But he bears watching."

"He does," Cowboy said.

"We're on it," Trent said. Cowboy assumed he referenced the remaining HIS agents.

"Thanks." He indeed was thankful Trent had been available to help him navigate this mess because his mind remained tied up with LizzyBeth.

He wondered how Trent functioned when Kelly had been in danger. Heck, LizzyBeth wasn't in trouble, and he couldn't focus on the ranch as a whole.

"How's Doc?" Cowboy asked. "Any new word?" He had left the hospital, leaving Ballpark behind to coordinate with the doctors and keep an eye on Doc. The two men were close friends, so it had been easy for Ballpark to agree to the mission. Ballpark would contact Trent with any news so Cowboy could focus—*ha ha*—on the ranch.

"Doc's awake and irritable." Trent chuckled. "They say doctors make the worst patients."

Doc wasn't a full-fledged doctor, but he was as close as they got on the teams. As a prior SEAL team operator and paramedic before that, Doc was their lifeline when out on ops. Was it only a couple of days ago Cowboy was hit on a mock op and Doc had no time to help him? That seemed ages ago.

"Good," Cowboy said. He looked at his watch. Too late to bother LizzyBeth as it was nearing Ethan's bedtime. If she left the room after, he would catch her. Yes, he would be listening for her door to open. *Stalker much?* he asked himself.

The men exchanged good nights and headed to their respective rooms. Cowboy needed a shower, and a cold one might be in order if he didn't quit thinking about the afternoon with LizzyBeth.

On his way to his room, the object of his thoughts exited her room. She quietly closed the door behind her, probably not to wake the little tyke. Cowboy stood frozen in the hallway.

She turned, saw him, and stopped. They stared at each other from about twenty-five feet separation. Even at that distance, he could see the change in her expression. Thank goodness it wasn't a look of embarrassment from their earlier activities. He had worried she would second-guess her actions since someone had almost caught them in the act.

"Hi, LizzyBeth," he said in a low voice as not to wake Ethan or alert anyone else.

"Hi," she said in an equally low voice.

He moved toward her with the intent of grabbing her up in his arms. Except she held up a hand to halt his progress.

"Stop," she said. "I don't want Ethan to know."

That stung his ego. Then he realized LizzyBeth wasn't saying no. Hell yeah! "My room?" he offered, full of hope.

She nodded, and his soul lifted. He held out his hand, and she grasped it, following him to his room.

This time there would be no interruptions.

23

INSIDE COWBOY'S ROOM, Elizabeth whispered, "I can't stay long. I need to be there if Ethan wakes." She felt guilt for leaving her son alone in a strange house, but he slept, and she needed Cowboy.

"I don't know about that," Cowboy said. "I don't think I can do fast with you."

"You don't have a choice," she said. "That is if you want me now." She would die if he said no, not after she had gotten her nerve up to come to him. The afternoon tease had convinced her she could do this.

"I guess I'll take what I can get," he said in a gruff voice.

"Good." She tugged her shirt over her head. "Get undressed."

Cowboy halted her hand as she went for her jeans. "Hold on there, darlin'. I want to undress you at least."

"This, darlin'," she stressed with a twang, "is called a quickie, you know, like a nooner."

"Why must it be that?" he asked.

"You're wasting time." She went for the zipper of her

jeans. "Ethan is asleep in a strange house, and your entire family is here. I won't get caught sneaking out of your room."

He pulled his shirt over his head. "I don't see how any of that dictates it must be a quickie." Yet he went for the zipper on his jeans, quickly removing them.

"When we're alone, we'll make it more of a special deal. I'll get a sitter for Ethan, and we won't be in your family home with half a dozen other people." *Did I just agree to another time?*

"My family won't care. If we ask Mom to watch Ethan, she would."

Mortified, she stopped unhooking her bra. "Don't you dare!"

"What? She would."

"Then she would know what we're doing."

"Darlin'," he drawled, "I believe she thinks we already are."

Elizabeth felt heat rise to her cheeks. "No, no, no. They can't know." How mortifying? Sure, they were adults, but still, in his parent's house felt juvenile.

Cowboy put his hands on his hips. "Why not? My brother and his wife have sex in the house, and Mom doesn't mind."

"They're married, you buffoon."

"Buffoon?" He laughed. "What happened to Captain America?"

She unhooked her bra and heard him draw in a breath. She looked up and saw the desire burning in his eyes.

"Quickie," she reminded him.

"Quickie." He nodded. "I'll agree, but only this once, and then at noon every day. I can't afford to miss that afternoon delight."

She laughed. Who else but Cowboy would call it that? She could fall hard for his man, but she refused to allow herself that unnecessary pain.

When she went to remove her panties, he stopped her with a hand. "At least let me unwrap the rest of you."

She nodded and allowed him to pull her undies down slowly. He slid to his knees while he did it and kissed the apex of her thighs. She shook down to the core. Her burning for this man ignited into a fireball that she knew needed to be extinguished in a hurry. Or she would burn for all eternity for this man.

"Up," she commanded. "Let me."

It took him a moment, but he finally stood and allowed her access to his clothing. She slid his underwear down, maneuvering over his hard, thick cock. Dadgum, Cowboy was much larger than Sean. She knew she shouldn't compare the two, but that had been all she had known for years.

Could she handle all of him? She almost laughed. She had read that in romance books and thought it hokey, but she knew the writers had some experience she hadn't had, until now after seeing Cowboy.

She wrapped her hand around him as much as she could and rubbed from base to tip, watching him toss back his head and groan. Then she froze, thinking about the noises they were making.

"Kiss me," she said. "Keep kissing me so we can be quiet." Boy, she was being bossy, but someone had to take control if she expected to get back to her son and out of here before his mother knew.

Cowboy narrowed his eyes at her, then nodded. Leaning down, he took her mouth with his in a hunger that matched her own. Their tongues dueled for dominance as their hands roamed each other's bodies—definitely quickie moves.

Slowly, he maneuvered them to the bed, and they toppled down, breaking their kiss briefly with the thud they made. Elizabeth's eyes widened at the noise, and he grinned. Retaking her mouth, he cupped her breast. Kneading it and tweaking the nipple sent errant electricity charges straight to her core. He had just added more kindling to the fire.

Elizabeth reached down and grasped his cock. It throbbed in her hand, and she knew he was as hot for her as she was for him. Elizabeth wished they had time to play. She would love to go down on him, taking as much of him as she could in her mouth and swallowing all of him as he came in her mouth. But not now.

"I need you, Cowboy," she whispered when they came up for breath.

He slid his hand down her belly to reach her pussy. She knew she was ready for him.

"You're so wet for me."

"I don't want to wait any longer," she cried in a low voice.

"I don't either." Cowboy reached over Elizabeth to his bedside table and pulled out a drawer, grabbing a row of condoms.

Elizabeth wasn't going to break their current path to ask

why he had so many condoms at his mother's home, but she was curious.

He tore one packet free, ripped it open, and rolled on the condom. Elizabeth loved watching that but belatedly felt she should have helped. *Next time.*

Taking her mouth with his once more, he held his cock and slid it to her center. Slowly, inch by inch, he slid into her, rocking with each move. Each new depth brought a wave of pleasure flowing through her body, from her toes to her head. It had been too long since she'd had sex.

When he was finally seated—yes, he did fit—they broke the kiss and gazed at each other. A fire burned in his eyes. Elizabeth reckoned it matched what she felt in her gaze.

Slowly, he withdrew a bit and rocked back into her until they found a rhythm that added wind to the fire inside her, igniting it into a brushfire. Oh, how she wanted it to continue until it burned all of her, consuming her in its wake, but they couldn't have a long lovemaking session this time.

She caught that she'd thought "this time" again. So, this wouldn't be her only time to climb into Cowboy's bed. They would have to plan better so they could spend hours. Maybe she should ask Deidra to sit for her. No, she couldn't do that as it would be too embarrassing.

He shifted, and she ignited into a ball of fire. She moaned, and he kissed her just in time to catch the noise leaving her throat. Good grief, this lovemaking felt incredible. With his hardness sliding in and out of her heat, sending wave after wave of fire through her veins, she didn't think she could stand more. Her body tingled in gratification from her toes to the tip of her head.

Then the climb began—the rise to putting out the flames. Elizabeth wanted that release so severely, and he had built her fire into a wild ride that wasn't forgiving in its pleasure.

She wrapped her legs around his thighs and pulled him deeper. He groaned in her mouth, and they rocked a few more times before her release came in waves, like water gushing to put out the flames. She floated for a moment, barely feeling him pump into her a few more times before he jerked and stilled.

Cowboy broke the kiss, lifted himself, and collapsed at her side, exhaling loudly.

They both breathed hard from the exertion. Even with the quickie, tiny beads of sweat had formed on their bodies. It had been hot and wildly erotic.

"I think I'm dying," she said.

"Not before me," he countered. He popped up on his hand, his arm bent at the elbow. "Boy howdy, that was mighty fine, pretty lady," he said in his best southern drawl.

Elizabeth rolled her eyes. "I bet you say that to all the ladies."

He looked hurt. "I've might said it a time or two, but no one has felt as good as you did. We were made for each other." His expression changed to one of near horror. Had he realized what he had said? She had and wasn't sure he meant it.

"I've got to get back to Ethan." Best to leave it now. Words were for another time when emotions were not in turmoil from hot and heavy sex.

"Stay," he pleaded.

"I'd love to, but I can't." She stood from the bed and dressed quickly.

He stood and removed the condom, tossing it in the garbage.

She dropped her head back and sighed. "Please tell me your mother doesn't empty your garbage." She looked at him for his response.

Cowboy grinned. Oh, she loved that crooked grin. "She doesn't."

"Thank goodness for small wonders." Dressed, she walked back to Cowboy and put her arms around his neck. "I'm sorry it's only a quickie."

"I'm not. I'll take what I can get. But you do owe me a marathon-length adventure."

She smiled. "Oh, I do, do I?"

"Yes." He kissed her hard, then swatted her on the butt. "Go before I rip those clothes back off you."

She opened his door a crack and peeked out. After seeing no one, she slipped out the door and closed it quietly behind her. When she got to her bedroom door, she opened it silently to find a still sleeping Ethan.

Elizabeth sat in the chair beside the bed, thinking how terrible a mother was to run off for a quickie while her son slept in the other room. It had never bothered her when she and Sean had sex with Ethan down the hall, but things were different.

Yet, she couldn't stop the smile of pleasure on her face. "So worth it," she whispered to the night.

24

THE FINAL DAY before the guests arrived had flown, and Cowboy had had no private time with LizzyBeth. They had all gone to bed exhausted, barely eating dinner, and he hadn't wanted to pull her from Ethan again. Having an affair with a single mother wouldn't be easy, and he would have to invest in babysitters. Maybe he could add Ethan to the HIS kids when Ballpark watched them. It was a funny thought.

The CEOs were due any minute. Everyone on the ranch had worked until late preparing. With Spencer under constant observation, no sabotage had occurred. Maybe they were wrong about the man. But Cowboy leaned to the side of caution.

If only they could get a lead on why someone had shot at the men. The agents were combing the range and had yet to find anything happening to warrant such a warning. To ensure the guests were not at risk, they had rerouted the trail ride to avoid that part of the range. Cowboy doubted the same thing would occur, but again, caution.

"Everything's ready," Deidra said as the group of workers and family huddled around the living room of the ranch house. "The guests are due to arrive in ten minutes."

The agents of HIS, minus Cowboy, had acted as the shuttle service and drove their rented SUVs to the airport to pick up the guests. Cowboy hoped the CEOs hadn't expected limo service to a dude ranch as he would never agree to that level of service because he considered it pretentious.

"We're expecting William and Regina Bond, along with their daughter Jessica," Jasmine said, "He's the CEO of Carhale Industries, with over 12,000 employees. Robin Strong and his partner, Evan Chance, are from Cattington Academy, with over 11,000 staff. And, finally, Steve Carruthers and Alex Green, CEO and COO of Mineco, Inc, with over 16,000 employees. The CEO of The Little Things had to cancel but asked to reschedule." She took a breath. "I've coordinated with them, and if they're satisfied with their experience, they'll book their leadership teams immediately. We are also discussing employee retreats. This event could be big for us, so please don't screw it up."

Mineco, Inc. Cowboy didn't like oil prospectors on his property. His mind stopped on that thought. Oil prospectors. Could it be that simple? But who would be prospecting? No. That didn't seem plausible, yet he couldn't let go of the thought. Maybe it was because the two executives were guests. Nick hadn't mentioned Mineco making an offer on the property, but they could have done it through a different company under their umbrella. He would find out if they had. That, someone could take to the bank.

"Does everyone have the schedule?" Jasmine looked around, and all nodded.

Cowboy glanced down at the sheet of paper she had handed him earlier. His primary assignment was to lead the trail ride, and he also had to show off breaking a horse and roping a calf. *Oh, the joy.* He hadn't wanted to come home and be part of the show, but Jasmine had convinced him his participation would help demonstrate the authentic cowboy experience for their guests. Besides, Nick couldn't perform, so Cowboy was stuck in his place.

The group rushed outside when an alert sounded that someone had passed through the main gate. Cowboy glanced at LizzyBeth, who had agreed to help the women cook and serve food, even though an official chef had started that morning. God, he missed her. It had only been a day since he had her in his bed, and it seemed like forever ago. Yet, he remembered the feel of her soft skin and the taste of her lips. He needed her again. This time, nice and slow.

Damn, he needed to shift himself, but he was in public. Hopefully, no one noticed he was sporting semi-wood just thinking about LizzyBeth naked in his arms. He almost chuckled at his "welcome" to the guests.

The SUVs arrived with little fanfare. The ranch hands opened doors and grabbed luggage. Jasmine had already communicated who rode in what vehicle and the cabin they were assigned. He had to hand it to her; she had her shit together. They would never have gone this route without her. He prayed it worked. The ranch was riding on it.

Cowboy also hoped Jasmine and Nick would work

things out. If she stopped flirting with everyone, that would help, but he couldn't worry about his brother's problems now. He glanced at Nick, hunched over the crutches, brooding at Jasmine. His brother had it bad. How had he never noticed that growing up? Maybe because he had been so gooey-eyed over her himself. She was a beautiful woman.

Jasmine and Cowboy stepped forward. He hated taking what should have been Nick's spot to welcome the guests, but Nick didn't want to greet them with his broken leg and crutches. Nick planned to stay in the background this go-round and evaluate their services. At least he was sober, and Cowboy considered that a significant plus in the brother column.

"Welcome to the Rockin' T Ranch," Jasmine said. "We're glad to have you."

Cowboy and Jasmine shook hands with each guest and exchanged names. Jessica, the daughter of the Bonds, fluttered her eyelashes at him and didn't want to let go of his hand. *Oh boy.* They didn't need someone like that with all the ranch hands and agents. Trouble with a capital T, he wanted to report. They needed a "no sleeping with the guests" rule for their employees and the independent contractors hired to work the ranch. Maybe Jasmine had thought of that, but he would suggest it if not. He would warn the men to keep it in their pants, reminding them this little filly was jailbait.

Cowboy introduced the rest of the family. Hands were shaken, and "Nice to meet you" was said.

"We're all here to make your experience authentic. Anything you need, just ask," Jasmine said. "The hands have taken your luggage to your cabins, and we've prepared a welcome luncheon for you in the common area."

Cowboy and Jasmine led the group to the common area in the middle of the grounds that transformed into a luncheon area, meeting room, and dance hall. Sometimes they converted it to all three in the same day.

While he socialized with the guests, his mind went to the other cabins that needed a few more things to be ready. They had twenty altogether, but they'd prepared only five for these guests. The others required minor work but mostly new roofing from the last major storm that blew through. He would see if Elizabeth would stay on longer to help get those cabins ready. That meant he would have to remain here also, but it would be worth it to be near her and, yes, near Ethan.

Cowboy heard Ballpark call him in his earpiece that connected him to the HIS agents. "Cowboy, we have a problem."

He excused himself from Mr. and Mrs. Bond and their clingy daughter. "What's the problem?" he asked Ballpark.

"We have an unexpected guest. A Mr. Sean Howe, and he says he's Elizabeth's husband."

A liar, just like Jasmine had been when she had introduced herself. Cowboy seethed. Had LizzyBeth invited her ex-husband to his ranch? Sean had no business here. Then his mind remembered Ethan, and Cowboy guessed he did have business here after all.

25

ELIZABETH FUMED WHEN her ex-husband showed at the ranch—as if a flirty teenager hadn't been enough. She would have a long talk with her mother for telling him where she and Ethan were visiting, because that was the only way he could have found out where they were.

Well, she wasn't really visiting; she had a job. Sure, she had completed all the tasks assigned before the guests arrived and could have left, but Cowboy had asked her to remain if something happened while the guests were in residence. Since she needed the money and wanted to be close to Cowboy, she had agreed. Ethan was having the time of his life with the horses and attention from everyone, and Elizabeth wasn't ready to take that away from him. Besides, she hoped Cowboy might warm to her son and take them as a package deal—well, if things continued to grow between them into what Elizabeth desired. She could see them, eventually, as a family. Then again, anyone she dated had to have that prospect, or she couldn't date them.

Mind, she and Cowboy were not dating. They were

having sex. Only the once, but she knew it would be more when they could squeeze it into their hectic schedules. But what happened when they returned to the real world? She couldn't fathom, only hope.

Dealing with her real world, she greeted her ex-husband. "Sean," she said, not too kindly, "what're you doing here?"

Sean narrowed his eyes at her. "I came to see you and my son."

"I'm working." She seethed at his audacity to walk on her jobsite. "This is not appropriate."

With her impeccable timing, Jasmine walked up to them and held her hand out to Sean, ignoring the scowling Cowboy and Ballpark. "Hello, I'm Jasmine Vaughn."

He shook her hand. "I'm Sean Howe."

"Howe? As in related to Elizabeth?" Jasmine asked.

"I'm her husband."

"Ex-husband," Elizabeth corrected.

Jasmine looked between the two with a calculating look in her eyes. "Well, it just so happens we have an open guest cabin. Would you like to stay? Free of charge, of course, since you're practically family to our Elizabeth."

The little bitch. *Our Elizabeth, my ass*. She was doing this to make Cowboy jealous. She wanted him to herself, even though she had Nick.

"No," Elizabeth said before anyone else could respond. "He's not staying."

"Yes, I would like to stay and see my son," Sean said and smiled as if that were a reasonable request. Which, in all honesty, it was, if she wasn't on a frickin' job.

"Will you excuse us, please?" she said to Jasmine and the agents.

The woman nodded, smirked, and walked away. "I'll get the key for you," she said over her shoulder.

Elizabeth and Jasmine had tolerated each other while finishing the preparations for the guests. Now, though, it looked like Jasmine had her claws back out. Was one man not enough for her? She had to have both brothers eating out of her hand?

Elizabeth moved away from Cowboy and Ballpark before speaking. "You're not staying. I'm working here."

"Perfect. It lets me spend time with Ethan because you can't watch him if you're working."

True, but she had the Vaughn women to watch over their son. Would they have time now that the ranch was in operation? She hoped so, but then again, she would have the time since she was only on standby for emergencies.

Jasmine returned with a key in one hand and Ethan holding the other. *The scheming little hussy.*

"Daddy," Ethan screamed, dropping Jasmine's hand. He raced to his father, who picked him up and swung him around. Ethan giggled, and Elizabeth felt two feet tall. But, by gosh, she was on the job. It wasn't a family retreat.

"Thanks," she said to Jasmine before snatching the key from her. She knew Cabin Five was vacant because one CEO had canceled, but she should put Sean in one of the unfinished cabins with a leaky roof.

Sean put Ethan down and held his hand, and the big idiot smiled as if he had won.

"Mr. Cowboy," Ethan said excitedly, "this is my daddy."

Cowboy nodded to Sean but didn't speak. Sean reached out his hand for a handshake and was left holding his hand alone, and he retracted it and eyed Cowboy.

Sean would fail to take Ethan away from her, which she knew was his primary intent. This trip was another attempt to show her as an unfit mother who ignored her son and jumped from bed to bed, or whatever he could use to win full custody. Joint custody wasn't enough for him, and Sean wanted to punish her for not returning to him and becoming a family once again.

"Let's go," Elizabeth said more harshly than she meant to. She might be mad at Sean, but she didn't have to lower herself to be mean. "This way," she said more gently.

"This is a great place," Sean said, walking beside her, still holding Ethan's hand.

Ethan let go and ran between them, grabbing both their hands. "Swing," Ethan said.

So, like all parents, the two swung Ethan as they walked. Their talk would wait until Ethan slept.

They reached Cabin Five, where she had almost made love to Cowboy, and she unlocked the door. She thought the Rockin' T should switch to keycards, but who was she to judge the authentic experience? She had never been to a dude ranch before this.

"Here you go." She ushered them into the cabin.

Sean whistled. "Nice digs for a ranch."

Elizabeth wrinkled her brows. What had he expected, the bunkhouse? "It was ready for a CEO. You may as well enjoy the care package." The women had put together the packages to include fruit, snacks, and wine. Even though she would rather not give it to Sean, there was no sense in letting the work go to waste.

"Thanks, Liz," he said, using the nickname he had given her. She hated it, and she had grown to love LizzyBeth. "Mind if Ethan hangs out with me for a while?"

Elizabeth did but said otherwise. "I'll be back in a couple of hours. Don't you dare leave with him."

"I wouldn't dare," Sean said.

She nodded and left the cabin, her tummy full of knots. She didn't trust her ex-husband. Luckily, the agents had gathered and waited near the cabin for her. When she approached them, Speedy asked, "Do we watch him?"

She wanted to hug the big man. "Please do. I don't want him leaving with Ethan."

"Will do," Romeo said.

"I'll walk you back to the house," Cowboy said.

She wouldn't argue with that. She needed to be in Cowboy's presence, to pull from his strength and calm. "I'm sorry he showed up."

"Don't be." He reached over and grabbed her hand. She almost fought it in case Sean watched but instead clasped her hand in his. It felt warm, loving, and supportive. She remembered him skimming his hands down her body in their rush to explore and pleasure each other.

"We'll keep an eye on him. You find out why he's here. I don't like it." Cowboy squeezed her hand.

"I know why he's here. He wants Ethan. He said before

147

he would sue for full custody, proving me an unfit mother."

Cowboy stopped. "What? You're about the best mother ever."

She thought of leaving her son to have a quickie with Cowboy. "Not always," she mumbled.

Cowboy reached out with a finger and lifted her chin. "You're a marvelous mother. Otherwise, you would have left him with your mother for this job."

Elizabeth knew she was a good mother. Like all parents, she screwed up occasionally, but she loved her son, and he came first in her life. That was why Elizabeth suddenly knew nothing could come from being with Cowboy except sex. He would never think as she did for the future—a future as a family. She hoped but knew down in her heart it was a hopeless dream.

She dropped his hand. Why was she messing around with him then? Sean was right. She wasn't the best mother out there.

"What?" Cowboy asked.

"I can't do a fling with you, Cowboy. I want to. Boy, do I want to, but I can't. My son is too important to me. If you wanted kids and to settle down someday, that would be different. But you've told me you don't want either. We can't continue." It crushed her heart to say that, but she had to. No more fooling herself into believing differently.

"Son of a—Don't let him dictate your life. He can't prove you an unfit mother because you aren't one. You're allowed to live a life, LizzyBeth." Cowboy reached for her hand again, but she pulled it away.

Her eyes watered at his calling her LizzyBeth. She would miss it. "After the trail ride, we're going home." Knowing she did what was right, she turned and walked away from him, taking short memories and a broken heart.

26

THE DAY OF the trail ride loomed closer each day. Cowboy's mood hadn't improved since LizzyBeth had told him she would leave after the event, and she had only stayed, or so his mother had warned him, because she had agreed to be on the chuck wagon. At least Jasmine wouldn't be going on the trail. That was a plus. He had noticed she hadn't flirted with all the guests or, come to think of it, with him lately.

The guests had spent the day prior examining the grounds, skeet shooting, and watching Cowboy's demonstrations—where Cowboy had fallen off a horse, not on purpose. Jasmine and Cowboy met with the guests to learn more about their desires for their employees. It appeared the ranch would make the balloon note after all.

If only Jessie would quit following him around and flirting. Christ, the girl was only sixteen, but she dressed and acted like a grown woman. Her parents ignored her overt flirting, and it annoyed the crap out of Cowboy. After he had tried to be polite to the girl, Rick, his ranch manager, had warned him, "Just 'cause trouble comes visiting doesn't mean you have to offer it a place to sit down."

Rick was always good with an old cowboy phrase. In regards to Cowboy's relationship with LizzyBeth, Rick had said, "Letting the cat outta the bag was a whole lot easier than putting it back." He figured it was good they never officially "let it outta the bag" since she planned to leave him and the ranch.

When Jessie reappeared, Cowboy beat it for the ranch house, seeking out his brother. When he found him in the office, Cowboy dropped into the chair opposite the desk. "Hey, Nick. Whatcha doin'?"

"Double-checking the books." As if to prove it, Nick slid the ledgers aside to clear the desk in front of him. "What's up?"

"Many things," Cowboy said. "First, what's up with your marriage?" He had avoided the topic too long. "Second, why aren't you out there with the guests?" *Let Jessie snuggle up next to someone else.*

Nick straightened. "My marriage is none of your business. Besides, Jasmine prefers things as they are."

"I doubt it. I've seen Jasmine look longingly at you."

Eyebrows rising in interest, Nick asked, "You have?"

"Christ, what is wrong with you two? If you want your marriage and your wife to quit acting like she's loose, then man up and be the husband in your relationship."

"Don't call my wife loose." Anger roared in Nick's features and words.

"Then stop her flirting. Did you know she told everyone

in Baltimore she was my wife?"

"No." Nick took a deep breath and sighed, looking defeated. "I don't know where we went wrong."

"Find out and fix it. Jasmine lives here with Mom and Becca, so let things be civil."

"Speaking of Becca," Nick said, changing the conversation, "she's got the hots for Jasmine's brother."

"Franklin?"

"Yeah, they've been dating, sort of."

Cowboy wiped a hand over his weary face. "Why has no one told me? I guess that would explain his hanging around since I've been here."

"He started hanging around about the time things started going wrong."

Straightening in his chair, Cowboy asked, "Do you think…?"

Getting his drift, Nick shook his head. "No. He offered to loan me the money or buy me out if it came down to the bank taking it. But that was after I told him of the other offers."

"To me, he offered to buy the place if we got in a jam. Tell me about the other offers." He had heard of them from the agents, but he wanted Nick's take.

"All oil prospectors. I think Mineco is one, even though they used a different company for the offer."

"Is that why Jasmine has them here?" Cowboy couldn't believe they would have invited oil prospectors to their ranch as guests.

"No, she doesn't know they offered for the property.

They called us to visit ahead of their employees, and it's what gave Jasmine the idea in the first place."

So, she hadn't thought of it all alone. That little minx. At least she found the idea and ran with it, and that was more than Nick had been doing.

"I don't like them here," Cowboy said. Ranchers hated oil prospectors on their land.

"I don't either," Nick agreed.

"Then why aren't you out there watching them?"

Nick pointed below the desk. "This leg."

"Bullshit. You get around just fine. It should be you, not me, beside Jasmine. I'm not staying, brother. I'm outta here as soon as we have a way to pay the note." That meant even if he had to empty his savings account. He wouldn't allow his mother and sister's home to go to the bank, leaving them homeless.

"I know," Nick admitted. "I just thought you might enjoy it and stay."

Cowboy snorted in disbelief. "Why would you want me to stay?"

"Because Mom blames me for running you off."

"It took two for that tango," Cowboy said gruffly. He and his brother had never spoken of this, and hell, this trip was the first they had spoken since he had left the Rockin' T for boot camp. It was past time they cleared the air.

"I'm sorry, Mike. I can't regret it because I have always loved Jasmine. I do hate that it broke up our friendship and family," Nick said.

Cowboy found it hard to hold grudges. The one with

his brother and Jasmine had been the longest, and it had also been the most profound wound to his pride and heart. Too much ugliness existed with grudges, and he refused to allow them to rule his actions. "I can't forget, but you're forgiven."

There, just like that, his heart lightened. He couldn't say he could forgive Jasmine so easily since she had been his wife at the time, but his brother had been a fool in love.

"That's it?" Nick asked.

"That's it." Then Cowboy thought of an idea. "That is if you patch things up with Jasmine. I'd hate to think I forgave you for nothing." He smiled at his brother—Lord, how he had missed the man in his life.

"I'm not sure how."

"Be a man, for one thing," Cowboy instructed him. "Get out there and be the man of the ranch. Show her you can do this with her. This ranch isn't even her ranch, and she has more vested in it than most of us."

"But my leg?"

"Excuses, excuses. You can walk with your crutches. The guests won't mind moseying on their vacation rather than always on the run." At least he expected so.

"Okay, I'll do it."

Cowboy nodded and left the office. One problem down. Too many more to go.

27

ELIZABETH WISHED SHE hadn't agreed to remain for the trail ride, which was originally a wagon trail ride, but since only the men wanted the adventure, it became a trail ride. The women wanted the spa treatment Jasmine had scheduled for them. For this group, they could only accommodate one massage at a time, but the women didn't mind waiting their turn.

She saw Sean stroll out of Cabin Five. She wanted him out of here, which would only occur when she left. Admittedly, Elizabeth liked watching Sean and Ethan with the horses, and Sean loved that little boy. She couldn't ask for more from a divorced parent, but she didn't trust him.

Steve Carruthers and Alex Green of Mineco, Inc. approached LizzyBeth. "How much of the land will we see on this trail ride?" Steve asked.

"I don't know." She smiled. "This will be my first time going on a ride with the ranch, but I hear we'll cover a lot of land."

"What will you be doing? Will you be herding cattle

with the men?" Alex asked with a wry smile.

"No." She laughed. "I'd fall off my horse too often. I'm riding with the chuck wagon. We figured you'd want to eat along the way."

"Hello, LizzyBeth," Cowboy said as he walked up. "Green. Carruthers." He nodded to the men. "Are you all ready for the trip?"

The men shuffled their feet. "Sure am," Steve said.

"They asked about how much land we'd cover," Elizabeth offered.

Cowboy narrowed his eyes at the men, and she couldn't understand why. "I bet they did."

Alex held his hands out, palms to Cowboy. "We're not here for trouble, and we truly want to see the land."

"We won't accept your offer," Cowboy spit out.

Elizabeth stiffened. What the heck was going on with these men? She had never seen Cowboy so rude, and it surprised her he would be so with guests.

"We rescinded our offer this morning," Steve said.

Cowboy straightened in surprise. "What?"

Still reeling from a conversation she couldn't follow, Elizabeth said, "Excuse me, men," and walked away.

Spotting Ethan with Deidra, she headed in that direction. When she reached them, she squatted down to Ethan's level. "Do you promise to be good for Ms. Deidra and your daddy?" She hated leaving Ethan behind and didn't trust Sean, but the two had talked in depth about this job. Sean had agreed to watch Ethan without bringing it up in court, and he stated he might not sue for full custody after all.

Something had changed in him, and she had no idea what or why. He had been so adamant about taking her to court for full custody. Now, he said he could live with joint custody assuming she didn't bar him from seeing his son. She had never stopped him from seeing Ethan, and she never would.

To ensure Sean didn't abscond with Ethan, Romeo told her he would also remain behind to keep an eye on Sean, and she appreciated the agent.

"Yes, Mommy," Ethan said. "Why can't I come with you?"

She wanted to use the not old or tall enough excuse, but those things only hurt a child's ego. "Mommy's going to be working and can't watch you."

"What about Mr. Cowboy? He could watch me."

Oh no. Ethan had gotten attached. She hoped Sean's attention helped the boy heal the wound she would soon create by leaving. "We'll all be busy. Besides, your daddy wants to spend time with you. Don't you want to ride a horse with him?"

"We can?" The boy's wide eyes showed his surprise and joy.

"Yes, we can, champ." Sean appeared from behind her. "We'll have all the ladies and horses to ourselves." He winked at Ethan.

Thank goodness Deidra had informed her that Nick would remain at the ranch and Franklin would check in to watch things. Otherwise, she would be freaked about leaving her son without Cowboy's supervision while he rode a horse, even with his father.

As she stood, her knees creaked, and she felt older than her thirty years. "Do you promise to be careful?" she asked Sean.

"Of course. I'd never risk Ethan's life."

Believing that, she nodded, leaned down, and hugged and kissed her son. "I'll be back in four days." She heard the typical trail ride lasted a week, but the CEOs asked for an abbreviated event. Oh, how she hated leaving Ethan, even for so few days.

Turning away, with her eyes shining with the tears she held back, she walked to the barn. Outside, Randy tightened the ties on the back of the covered wagon. They would ride ahead of the herd to find their preplanned spot to stop for lunch and then on to their evening sleeping spot. She liked they wouldn't be eating trail dust like the two men from Mineco. They had pulled drag duty first—eating the dust of the herd. After seeing Cowboy with them, she wouldn't rule out a rigged selection.

The cowboys and guests would move a small herd through Rockin' T land, then spend the night under the stars. It sounded romantic until Elizabeth thought of bugs. Lots of creepy, crawly bugs.

"Are you ready?" Randy asked her. "We need to get moving so we can get ahead of the herd."

Cowboy, Trent, Rick, Jorge, and Spencer each paired with a guest. Speedy and Ballpark would remain with the chuck wagon. Doc had been released from the hospital but couldn't travel, so he stayed at the ranch under Romeo's supervision.

They had an entire group to handle. Elizabeth wondered what the plan was when they had more guests. She'd heard Jasmine pleading for Nick to hire more ranch hands, so maybe that would work in the future.

With one last look at her son with his father, she climbed aboard the wagon and sat on the hard bench.

"Here." Randy handed her a cushion.

"Bless you," she said as she accepted it, then put it under her butt. Not great, but much better.

He chuckled. "It's a rough ride without it. Hell, it's a rough ride with it, but at least your butt will feel better."

Randy grabbed the reins, snapped them, and yelled, "Hiyyah."

The chuck wagon began to move, and the outriders—Speedy and Ballpark on horseback—rode up beside them.

"Are you ready to rough it?" Ballpark asked her.

"Not in the least," she shouted over the jangle of the harnesses on the horses. She mentally laughed at the thought of her snuggling up in the back of the chuck wagon instead of her sleeping bag on the ground. "Not in the least."

28

COWBOY HAD BEEN an Air Force Special Ops pararescueman, was an agent of HIS, and made and diffused bombs. Never, in all those days, had he worried so much about so many things. His mind whirred about whether they should have allowed the executives to arrive and participate since there was still trouble afoot. Yet, they had, so he had to go with it.

To make matters worse, LizzyBeth was out of his sight. He had left Speedy and Ballpark with her, and he trusted them and Randy, but he still worried. He wasn't a typical worrier, especially about others, so LizzyBeth on his mind mucked things up for him.

Trent watched Cowboy's CEO—Steve Carruthers—so Cowboy could maneuver through the small herd that the executives and his ranch hands moved through the range. The two agents had taken the executives from Mineco to keep an eye on them because Cowboy didn't trust them as far as he could throw them. They said they had rescinded their offer, but why? He hadn't asked and wished he had.

Cowboy watched Robin and Evan gaze at each other across the herd. Those two men had it bad. Of course, if LizzyBeth had been across the way from him, he would probably be looking at her with the same longing. He stared ahead at the dust the chuck wagon left behind. He would see her in a few hours. Maybe they could snuggle under the blankets tonight.

Wait, scratch that, she had said no to them. She planned to leave after the trail ride, so Cowboy had four evenings to convince her to stay with him. His palms sweated inside his gloves. She meant more to him than a bedmate, and he had to prove it to her. What about Ethan, though? They were a package deal.

Cowboy noticed Spencer and William Bond had switched to drag. Was Spencer their problem? The sabotage had stopped when HIS watched him, but that could have been a coincidence. What motive would Spencer have to try to destroy the ranch? It was his workplace, his home, but money spoke volumes.

Cowboy paired back up with Carruthers. "Having fun?" he hollered over the noise of the herd.

Carruthers wiped his forearm over his sweaty forehead. "Not really."

Inside, Cowboy laughed at the man's misery, and it served the old codger right. "Why'd you come then?"

They pulled their horses closer so they wouldn't have to yell.

"I thought it might be fun to herd cattle, but my butt is already sore," Carruthers said. "I'll stick to prospecting."

"Tell me why you wanted this property," Cowboy demanded.

Carruthers looked at him, then looked away. "Why do we want any property? The prospect of oil."

"Yet, you decided to pull your offer." Why would they offer without knowing for sure if there was oil? Had they been prospecting on the ranch and shot at his men?

"Well, your brother said he wasn't selling even an acre, and he wouldn't allow us to prospect, so we pulled our offer."

Good on Nick for standing up to the men. "Yet you stayed for this."

Carruthers nodded. "Alex wanted the experience, and he always wanted to be a cowboy, so we stayed."

Cowboy turned toward Alex Green and Trent. Green did appear to be having the time of his life while Trent just smiled and watched everything. Something told him Trent might turn his horse ranch into a small dude ranch. He'd loved the experience so much.

Ahead, Cowboy noticed the chuck wagon had stopped to serve them lunch, and he was hungry. Hungry for food and to see LizzyBeth. He turned to let the men know to stop the herd for lunch, but Trent must have noticed the chuck wagon also as he had started the process. Stopping a herd took space, but they had plenty between them and the chuck wagon. He worried about a stampede because the executives wouldn't be able to handle it, which could be deadly. The executives had already balked when they were required to wear protective headgear—insurance purposes,

Jasmine had said.

Jasmine had indeed done her homework on this entire experience. Dad would have been proud of what the business had become. With this success, they could expand for larger crowds and staff. The remaining work on the guest cabins would take maybe another week or two, and they would be ready for these executives' teams.

Once the herd settled, eating grass and drinking at the spring Randy had stopped near, the men who were not on herd watch hustled to the wagon. It was a cold lunch, but it was food, and herding cattle made one hungry. He imagined the executives never realized the work that went into riding a horse, and they would be sore in the morning. Maybe they should have brought the masseur with them. He chuckled at the idea of massages on the trail.

Then he thought of the massage LizzyBeth had given him, and his dick hardened. Damned uncomfortable riding a horse with a hard-on, so he dismounted and hoped no one noticed the wood in his britches.

Cowboy walked up to LizzyBeth, ignoring the other men. "Hey," he said with his best smile.

LizzyBeth looked up from what she was doing. "Hey, back." She didn't grace him with the smile she usually did after saying hello. It saddened him that she would really leave him—leave them. Of course, they were not "them" yet. Only bedmates. To be "them," he needed to accept Ethan, and while he liked the little cuss, he couldn't see him giving his heart to a child again. It still bled for his little girl.

Focused solely on LizzyBeth, Cowboy hadn't heard

Randy's approach.

"Boss, we've got a problem," Randy told him.

Great. "What?" They had only been on the trail half a day.

"One of the wheels is splintering."

"Didn't you bring a spare?" They always packed spares in wagons, did they not?

Randy nodded. "I have one, and we'll change to it now."

"So, what's the problem?"

"It looks like someone tampered with the wheel on the wagon."

Cowboy mentally cursed. How could that be? They had been watching Spencer, Carruthers, and Green, the three they suspected of mischief. Who had they missed?

"The problem," Randy continued, "is if something happens to this one, we're stuck. No spare."

Well, that just flat-out sucked. Cowboy thought it through before saying, "Since we're still close, we'll send back for a spare now, just in case."

"If I go back, there won't be dinner tonight," Randy unnecessarily informed him.

They didn't have much choice, because a horse couldn't carry a wheel due to its size. Then a thought struck Cowboy. "Pass out cold fare for tonight. After we get a new wheel on, LizzyBeth and I will take the chuck wagon back and pick up a spare. We'll meet you in time for a hot breakfast."

LizzyBeth looked up at him. "Me?"

"Unless you want to ride a horse with the herd," Cowboy said.

She paled. "No. I'll go back with you." While she verbally agreed, her body language seemed to disagree over being alone with him.

He didn't care. He would take every minute he could with LizzyBeth until he convinced her to stay. Then, they could continue having incredible sex until they were tired of each other and she and her son left. Hopefully, her ex had left the ranch by the time they arrived back from the trail ride.

Randy and LizzyBeth handed out the fare for the evening. Then he and Randy changed the wheel and switched places. Speedy and Ballpark decided to remain with the herd and the executives. Cowboy appreciated the help, even though Speedy was a greenhorn.

"Ready?" Cowboy asked LizzyBeth. "Need a hand?" He offered to lift her into the wagon, but she declined and climbed up independently.

Stubborn woman. Cowboy walked around the back of the wagon to climb in on his side. He had four hours alone with her before they reached the ranch, and he could do plenty of sweet-talking in that time.

29

"ARE YOU SURE you want to leave after the trail ride?" Cowboy asked Elizabeth on their ride back to the ranch.

"Yes," she answered—just the one word, nothing else. Cowboy hadn't asked for more, and she wouldn't offer it. She needed to distance herself from him physically and emotionally.

"Why?"

"I told you. I can't do an affair or Sean will declare me as an unfit mother." She shifted in her seat to put more space between them because she couldn't even stand to touch him. The electricity between them remained strong. "It has to be something more."

She guessed Cowboy had never done something more. Sure, he probably dated but never for longer than a few months. Boredom would generally set in, or he would notice someone new. Yeah, she knew his type, and it wasn't her, as she was someone in for the long haul.

Yet, Elizabeth wanted something more with Cowboy. Things felt different than they had with Sean. Even before she and Cowboy had made love that one time, all hot and heavy, she'd looked forward to working in his place, seeing him every day. God, her heart broke.

"Won't you at least stay and help us fix the rest of the place? It'll only be for another week or two," he asked.

Financially, she should. She didn't have work lined up, but emotionally, she could not. The longer she stayed around Cowboy, the more lost she would become. He would never want what she wanted. He would never want to be a family.

"It's time I go home." She also needed to get Sean out of here because he could only cause problems. Sure, it was good that he had time with Ethan, but she hated not trusting him to remain on the ranch with her son.

"LizzyBeth," Cowboy began, then took off his cowboy hat and resettled it on his head. "I want you to stay, not to fix the cabins, but to be with me."

He had gone and said it. Elizabeth groaned inside because she wanted to stay. Oh, how she wanted to stay, but she couldn't think of only herself. She had to think of Ethan first. Sure, she was allowed to have a love life, but one with Cowboy would only bring more heartache.

"I can't" was all she said.

No other conversation occurred on the remaining ride home. Still, Elizabeth enjoyed being with him, and that hurt her soul.

At the ranch, Romeo, Franklin, and Nick met them. In a near panic at not seeing Sean or Ethan, she asked, "Where's my son?"

Nick must have heard the worry in her voice. "It's okay.

He's with Mom and Becca."

Elizabeth jumped from the wagon and cringed over its impact through her body. She had to see her son and know he was safe.

*****

"WHATCHA BACK FOR?" Nick asked Cowboy as LizzyBeth moved away.

Cowboy jumped down from the wagon and watched her retreat. "Wagon wheel."

Franklin looked at both wheels. "They look fine to me."

"We need a new spare," Cowboy told the men. "One of the ones on the wagon splintered, and not by accident."

Nick swore. "But how?"

"I don't know," Cowboy said.

"We watched Spencer and those prospectors," Romeo said. "They didn't come near the wagon."

"I know." Cowboy looked around the ranch. "Where's Sean?" He didn't suspect the man of any sabotage on his ranch, but he wanted to know where the man who had once held LizzyBeth's heart was. He didn't trust the man not to win back his woman so they could be a family again. There he went with *his woman* again.

"He's in his cabin. He had some work to do, or so he said, so the women have Ethan," Nick said.

Cowboy admittedly missed the little tyke, and that surprised him. He had only been gone less than one day. Mentally, he shook his head. He couldn't worry about LizzyBeth and Ethan or Sean right now. He had to worry about the ranch and its problems. Someone was still sabotaging. Had Randy not noticed the wheel, someone may have been injured, and the trail ride would have had to return before schedule. The executives wouldn't enjoy that, and Jasmine would have his hide.

Nick continued, "He said he wanted to see you when you returned."

Cowboy couldn't be bothered with Sean now. He had a trail ride to catch. "Anything happening at the ranch?" Cowboy asked the men, glad Franklin had stayed to help.

"Doc's trying to get up and around," Romeo said.

"Did you tie him down?" Cowboy asked jokingly.

"No, I threatened to be his medic when he injured himself, and that made him stay down."

Cowboy chuckled. "What else? Any problems?"

Nick shook his head. "Nothing here."

"Good." Cowboy led the men to the barn and the wheels for the wagons. Thank goodness they had invested in more than one wagon and many wheels. He would use the same wagon but have a good spare. He believed the executives would excuse this little bump in the trail, so he didn't worry about business. But they had to get moving if they didn't want to be traveling by night. That was dangerous for the horses and the wagon.

"I want you to keep your eyes open," Cowboy told them. "Someone is messing with us and isn't done. Expect the worst to happen."

"Worse than the shooting?" Romeo asked.

Cowboy closed his eyes and sighed. They had been so

lucky on that front, and Doc and the horse would survive to see another day. He opened his eyes and gazed at each man as he said, "Just keep your eyes open."

Nick leaned on his crutches. "If you've got this, I'll head in and let Mom know what's happening."

"I'll go with you," Romeo said. "It's time to check on Doc."

That left Franklin with Cowboy. One extra hand was enough. "Go. We've got this," Cowboy said.

The men left, and Cowboy turned to Franklin. "Have you had any problems at your ranch?"

"Nothing," Franklin answered. "Except for the shooting, it sounds like someone is making mischief here."

"Sabotage is more like it," Cowboy said. "Someone wants us to fail."

"Why?" Franklin asked.

"So they can buy up the land." Cowboy just had to find out why they wanted his family's land.

"There's land for sale in the next town," Franklin said. "Why don't they just buy that?"

"Exactly," Cowboy said.

The men picked up the wagon wheel, prepared to lug it out to the wagon when Sean walked in, breathless.

"There you are," Sean said. Then he looked at Franklin and froze.

Cowboy drew his brows in. What was with those two?

Before he could speak, LizzyBeth entered the barn. "Are you ready to go back?" She froze when she saw Sean.

What is with these people? "No, we're not ready yet," he

told LizzyBeth. Then to Sean, he said, "I'm a little bit busy right now. Can this wait?"

Sean shook his head. "No. I need to speak with you privately."

That piqued his interest. "Okay, let me and Franklin load this wheel first." The damn thing had gotten heavy.

Sean cut a glance to Franklin, then nodded. "Okay."

Franklin dropped the wheel and snatched LizzyBeth to his front. With an arm around her neck, he held her tight to him, then pulled a gun from his pocket and pointed it to her temple.

"No, he won't talk with you alone," Franklin said.

30

COWBOY DROPPED THE wheel, and it landed on his foot. He ignored the sharp pain and remained still but ready. "What the fuck, Franklin?" Cowboy said, fear flowing through his veins for LizzyBeth, yet the calm he felt before disarming a bomb swept over him. "Let her go."

"It's him," Sean said unnecessarily. Cowboy had figured that out by the gun pulled on LizzyBeth.

Cowboy considered his options. He couldn't go for his handgun fast enough nor make the distance to LizzyBeth without chancing Franklin shooting her. "What do you want?" Cowboy asked, already guessing the answer.

"I want this land," Franklin said. "Or she gets it."

Cowboy didn't believe Franklin would shoot LizzyBeth, but Cowboy couldn't chance it either. "Done. Now, let her go." Had he just given away the family home and business for one woman? One woman who turned his world upside down. The one woman he loved. Loved? Nothing was more important than her and Ethan. Nothing. He would buy a new place for his mom and sister to live.

"No," cried LizzyBeth, fear lacing her eyes and anger mixed in her voice. "Don't do it, Cowboy. I'm not worth it."

"Yes, he will," added Sean. Then the idiot stepped closer to Franklin and LizzyBeth. "Now, let her go."

Before Cowboy saw his neighbor's intention, Franklin removed the gun from LizzyBeth's head and shot Sean in the gut. The blast rang loud in the barn. "Stay back!" Franklin yelled, veins bulging at his neck.

Cowboy moved toward a bleeding Sean, and Franklin pointed the gun at him. Cowboy froze.

"Leave him. I had plenty of time to ensure you didn't make the banknote before you sold the property to me."

So that had been the game—just as Cowboy figured.

"That mongrel," Franklin said, nodding toward Sean, "must've overheard me talking about the next step."

What the hell was the next step? Cowboy wasn't sure he wanted to know.

Franklin nodded toward Cowboy's weapon holstered at his side. "Now, slowly, with two fingers, pull your gun and toss it to me."

Cowboy watched blood ooze from an unconscious Sean's gut. Romeo would hear the gunshot and be here soon, so he hoped Sean could hold out. Seeing no other option, Cowboy did as Franklin said, only he didn't toss his gun all the way to Franklin. Cowboy threw it between them so he would have a chance to grab it before all hell broke loose. And hell would probably break loose when Cowboy figured out how to rescue LizzyBeth.

Holding his hands up in front of him in submission, Cowboy said, "Done. Now, I told you I'd give you the ranch. Tell me why." He needed to buy time for Romeo to get here, assess the situation, and eliminate the threat.

"Oil. Why else? You have it, and I don't," Franklin said.

It was that simple and that greedy. Cowboy should never have believed the Mineco executives. "Are you working with Carruthers and Green?"

"I was, but the assholes backed out at the last minute." Franklin sneered. "They like the idea of the dude ranch surviving. They were going to tell you about the oil, and I couldn't have that."

Did that mean he planned to do away with the two executives? "So," Cowboy said, never looking at LizzyBeth but remembering the fear he had seen in her eyes when Franklin had grabbed her, "you've been the one sabotaging our ranch, and you shot Doc and the horse."

"I'm sorry about the horse. Spencer did the shooting, and he never meant to hurt one of the animals." Franklin waved the gun at him. "Now, let's get inside and get that paperwork ready. I know an attorney who'll sign the transfer as soon as we get it to him."

"You're going to have to let LizzyBeth go before I do anything," Cowboy said. He had to get her free and get to Sean before the man bled to death. *Hurry, Romeo.*

"Not gonna happen," Franklin said, moving the gun back to LizzyBeth's temple.

This time, Cowboy did chance a glance at LizzyBeth. Her fear had turned to hatred and anger. *Good girl.* That helped him not worry about her being afraid. Yet, she should be in fear that Franklin's gun might go off on accident.

Cowboy crossed his arms over his chest and narrowed his eyes at Franklin. Romeo would be here by now, sneaking up behind Franklin. He had to have faith in his fellow agent. "If you go into the house with a gun to LizzyBeth's head, the women will freak out."

He wished LizzyBeth had been as trained as Kate Hamilton had been so she would drop and allow him to charge the threat. But Cowboy had to work with what he had. And what he had was an untrained civilian in danger and no explosives—not that they would be beneficial in this situation. He had to talk his way out of this situation diplomatically, and he wasn't a silver-tongued lad.

"No. I'll stay out here with Elizabeth while you and your brother have your sister sign the papers. Any sirens or funny business, and she gets it." Franklin pressed the gun deeper into LizzyBeth's temple, and Cowboy tensed. Accidents happened, and he couldn't afford for the gun to go off.

Franklin's plan of him going inside alone sounded all kinds of stupid to Cowboy. But he would play along since he didn't have the upper hand. "What happens if my brother and sister say no? They don't know LizzyBeth, and she may not be worth the ranch to them."

"Then you'd best convince them," Franklin roared.

Cowboy glanced at Sean and noticed the man's shallow breathing. Fuck. He had to get this moved along. *Hurry the fuck up, Romeo.*

"Say I convince my brother and sister to sign over the

papers, what makes you think we'll just let you walk out of here?" Cowboy asked.

"She comes with me," Franklin said.

"See," Cowboy said, "that doesn't work for me. Either you release her now and accept my gentlemen's promise to turn over the land, or we sit here until someone comes looking for us."

"No one's coming to look for you," Franklin spat. "They think you're leaving for the trail."

"They may have heard the shot," Cowboy said, realizing he shouldn't have said that.

In the next instance, Franklin grunted and fell. Romeo smiled at Cowboy.

Cowboy rushed forward to LizzyBeth, his heart in his throat. "Christ, Romeo, he had a gun to her head. What if you hadn't knocked him out or the gun went off?"

"I'm a pro at this shit," said the former FBI agent. Romeo rushed over to Sean to check on him. "His pulse is weak. We've got to get him to the hospital."

"Are you all right?" Cowboy asked LizzyBeth at the same time.

"I'm fine." LizzyBeth rushed in his arms, shaking all over. "Sean," she whispered in his ear.

Right. The ex. Cowboy pulled back and went to the other side of Sean, where Romeo had already started first aid.

"LizzyBeth," Cowboy said, "run to the house and tell them we need Doc out here. I'll call for Life Flight."

"All he did was try to save me," LizzyBeth said with tears streaming down her face.

Cowboy went to her and grasped both of her arms. "LizzyBeth." He shook her, and she seemed to notice him. "Go to the house and tell them we need Doc."

She nodded and dashed away.

Once she was out of earshot, Romeo told Cowboy, "You'd best get that Life Flight here fast. I don't know if he's going to make it."

While dialing 911, Cowboy's gut clenched, and he silently cursed. He couldn't allow Ethan to lose his father. Even though now, he knew he would do anything to be the boy's stepfather.

31

ELIZABETH PACED AT the hospital, her stomach in a tangle. She had no idea what she would tell Ethan if Sean died trying to save her, but she would make him a hero in her son's eyes. Now though, it would leave a large hole a child couldn't understand.

Cowboy had given her a ride after Life Flight had departed. The two had said maybe three words the entire drive. Her mind had been whirring on *what if Sean dies*? Not that she wanted to get back with him, but she didn't want her son to be fatherless. Sure, they didn't spend every day together, but the time they did spend together, Ethan enjoyed.

"LizzyBeth," Cowboy said and waited until she stopped and turned to him. "Why don't you sit a spell? Pacing isn't going to help move things along faster."

She knew that, only she couldn't sit still, especially beside Cowboy. "I'm fine." She turned and continued to pace in the nearly empty surgical waiting room. At least, it was almost empty in their corner, as it appeared everyone else had bunched up further from her and Cowboy.

Cowboy sighed loudly. "How about some coffee? Would you like some?"

Absently, she nodded. Not that she really wanted the coffee, but she wanted to be alone in her thoughts. If Sean survived, he would need care, and he had no one else but her. His family lived in Canada, and they might or might not fly down and help him. After meeting them, she doubted it, as it would interfere with his mom's social scene.

Was it wrong of her that she didn't want to take care of Sean? After all that he had put her through in their marriage, divorce, and later? Yet, who else would do it? No one. So, she would be stuck playing nurse.

How did she explain that to Cowboy? Why would she explain that to Cowboy? There would be no need. As much as it pained her, the two of them were not an item, and they never would be. Not with Ethan as her son. Cowboy wouldn't take them as a family. That burned her insides to the core.

"Here you go," Cowboy said as he handed her a warm cup of coffee. "It's hot, so be careful," he added unnecessarily.

She accepted the cup, noting it was a bit hot to the touch, then thanked him. "What do you think is taking so long?"

Cowboy shrugged. "It's a gutshot, and I imagine it takes more time."

Elizabeth blew on her coffee, then took a sip, and the liquid burned its way down her throat, her esophagus, and into her stomach. "Do you think...?" She stopped her thought because she couldn't ask if he thought Sean would die.

"I don't know," he answered anyhow. "I don't know." He tried to pull her to him for a hug, but she pulled back. She couldn't be that woman for him right now. Their time had passed.

A harried-looking man in green scrubs walked into the waiting room. "Family for Ethan Howe."

She turned, handed her coffee to Cowboy, and said, "I'm his wife," by mistake. Out of the corner of her eye, she saw Cowboy stiffen. "I mean, I'm his ex-wife," she corrected even though the doctor couldn't care less. "I'm the only family he has locally."

The doctor nodded. "He made it through the surgery." Then he said a bunch of medical stuff she didn't understand about lacerations and his bowel. "He's in the ICU. If he makes it through the night, we should be okay. But he's going to need extra care when he's released. Someone to take care of him, fetching things and such, as he won't be able to move around much at first."

"I'll do whatever it takes," she said.

The doctor nodded, turned, and walked away.

"Thank God," she said in an exhale. She hugged Cowboy, who juggled her hot coffee in one hand and put his other hand on her back. "He's going to be okay." Again, Cowboy stiffened, and she immediately pulled back. "I'm sorry. I just got excited."

He frowned, and her joy dimmed. She couldn't read him, but she guessed he hadn't expected her to hug him since she had said they were no more.

She continued as if it necessary to explain, "It was impulsive. I would have hugged anyone near me at the great news."

"Uh-huh," he said. "Did you want to stay, or would you like to come back tomorrow?"

Thinking that tonight she could only sit by his bedside for a few hours at a time, she said, "Tomorrow. I'll pack up Ethan and me, and we can stay in town until Sean is released. Then we'll take him home."

Cowboy's frown deepened. "Okay, let's go."

The long drive back to the ranch was tense. Elizabeth was unsure exactly why, but she guessed Cowboy disapproved of her helping Sean. Oh well, Sean was important to her son, so he had to have some importance in her life, even if she would prefer otherwise.

When they arrived back at the ranch, she quickly exited the SUV and hurriedly said, "Thank you," to Cowboy.

Deidra met her at the door. "How is he?"

"He'll survive," she said in relief and hugged the woman. Pulling away, she continued, "Ethan and I will go back tomorrow and stay with him until he recovers."

Deidra cocked her head to the side. "What about Mike?"

Elizabeth scrunched up her brows. "What about him? He drove me back. He's behind me?"

"No," Deidra shook her head. "What about you and my son?"

"Oh," she said. *What to say?* "There is no me and Cowboy," she said as he walked in the door.

"Good to know," he said and walked by her without another word.

What the heck? He acted like a spoiled child who had just lost his favorite toy, and he knew they were no longer together. Heck, she had planned to leave in the next couple of days anyhow. *The guests*, she suddenly remembered.

"Oh, Deidra, the guests, I completely forgot. Do you still need my help, or can you do without it?"

Deidra took her hand and patted it. "We'll be fine, dear. We hired on a couple of Franklin's hands, and they took the chuck wagon back out and are setting up the rest of the events."

Whew, that was a relief. "Okay, thank you. I'm going to talk to my son, explain things, and pack." She only hoped she didn't run into Cowboy again before she left because she didn't know what else to say to him except goodbye.

Elizabeth asked, "Deidra, can one of those hands drive Ethan and me into town tomorrow?"

Deidra looked down the hall toward Cowboy's room and nodded with a frown. "Sure, we can make that happen. Are you sure it's what you want to do?"

"I don't have a choice," she said. And she didn't. Sean was Ethan's father, and he needed a father in his life. And Cowboy said he would never be a father again, so they could never be together. It saddened her, but she had to look forward to the beauty of the memorable times they had spent together.

32

COWBOY WAS QUITTING all women. Well, at least women he deemed were "the one." LizzyBeth had walked away from him without a backward glance to take care of her ex-husband, of all people. Sure, the man had been shot trying to save her, but still, he was her ex-husband and her past, and Cowboy was supposed to be her future.

After he had decided he wanted to be a father to little Ethan, she left the ranch and Cowboy's life. That put a hole in his heart he doubted would ever heal.

Jasmine's big plan had been a success, and the ranch was doing well with his brother sober and in charge. Nick and Jasmine were in marriage counseling, and Cowboy wished them the best. The family was still discussing what to do about the oil. And, speaking of oil, Spencer had been slick as an eel in leaving the roundup before he could be apprehended.

"Cowboy," Boss said, "are you paying attention?"

He was not. The teams were briefing about an upcoming op, and he couldn't focus. "Sure thing, Boss," he lied. He wanted something to blow up, so he hoped they had to breach a building.

"You're not paying attention," Ballpark said in a low voice beside him.

Cowboy shook his head. "Sure I am."

"Hey, Boss," Ballpark said, "can we take a quick break?"

As if knowing Ballpark's reasoning, Boss agreed, and the briefing took a ten-minute break.

Once separated from the others, Ballpark asked, "You haven't called her, have you?"

"Why would I do that? She made her choice, and it wasn't me." He still couldn't believe she went back to her ex-husband after all the trouble he had caused her. Sean should be decently healed by now, but Cowboy imagined LizzyBeth still at his side.

"You're an idiot," Ballpark said. "You let the best thing that has happened to you walk away."

"Didn't you hear me say she made her choice?" Cowboy didn't need this discussion. His heart hurt enough without being reminded she had walked away and taken the little boy who had wormed his way into Cowboy's heart.

"Let's go blow some shit up," Ballpark suggested.

"Now you're talking my language." Cowboy smiled for the first time since LizzyBeth had left him.

* * * * *

WHEN COWBOY RETURNED home for the day, he

nearly panicked. There were sounds from his home as if someone were destroying it. He pulled out his Glock and turned the unlocked doorknob—which he had locked when he had left for the day. He should call the police, but this was his home. His domain. His responsibility to protect.

Another crash sounded, and he winced. What were they doing to his home? Why vandalize it? If his lock was that easy to pick, he needed a security system. Maybe Devon could design one for him as he had for others in the unit.

"It's about time you're home," the sweetest voice he had ever heard said. "I thought I was going to have to demo this kitchen by myself."

"LizzyBeth," he said as he holstered his weapon. "What are you doing here?" He looked around. "And why are you destroying my kitchen?" Cabinets had been pulled from the walls and were all about the floor.

She smiled beautifully. God, he missed her. "You hired me to remodel your kitchen. Don't you remember?"

He had but figured he would never see her again. "How did you get in?"

LizzyBeth winked. "Trade secret."

Trade secret his ass. Ballpark had left early, and he had Cowboy's spare key. The fucker had set this up and hadn't given Cowboy a clue.

What did this mean? Her being here, remodeling his kitchen? "How's your ex?"

"Oh"—she waved her hand in dismissal—"he's okay. He's getting around good enough now that he doesn't need my care."

He wondered to what extreme that care extended to but wouldn't ask. He really didn't want to know. He wanted LizzyBeth back and hoped this was a sign she wanted the same thing. Otherwise, why would she be here? *To pay her bills, maybe?*

"Come help," she said with a big grin. "Tearing down cabinets is a good workout for the body and mind."

Oh, he knew destroying shit helped his mind. Only, it was his shit, and he usually didn't waste his stuff.

"Why are you here, Elizabeth?"

She stopped and frowned. "That's the first time you've called me Elizabeth."

He shrugged, knowing he was distancing himself from her. She might do the work, but they couldn't jump back into bed, because he couldn't stand for her to walk away again. "That's your name."

"Yeah, but I prefer when you call me LizzyBeth."

So did he. "Why are you here?" he asked again.

She dropped the hammer in her hand and walked over to him. "I wanted to say I'm sorry for leaving the way I did, and I should have said goodbye and thank you for everything."

He nodded. At that time, he might not have let LizzyBeth go, and that was where he had failed because he hadn't hung on to her. "So, you decided destroying my kitchen was the next move?"

Laughing, she playfully swatted at his chest. He didn't even do the playact that it hurt because his heart was the thing hurting.

Noticing he wasn't playing along, she cleared her throat. "Well, I decided that if I could only have you for a fling, that would do."

He hadn't expected such blunt speech from her, but he liked it. "So, you're saying you came back and destroyed my kitchen so we could have sex?"

After dropping her brows, she bit her lip. "Well, if you put it like that, yes."

Laughter rang from his belly and up to his chest. Bless her heart, as his mom would say. He noticed she didn't laugh and stopped. "What if I no longer want a fling?"

Redness crept up her face. "Oh. I hadn't thought of that." She stepped back, turned, and looked at the mess in the kitchen. "I can fix it all."

With her back to him, he smiled broadly. She wanted him and would take a fling. Well, he had news for her—it was all or nothing. No more playing around. "I'd like that," he said about her fixing things. "I did hire you to remodel the kitchen, so by all means, do so."

She looked over her shoulder at him, hurt in her eyes, and turned back to the kitchen mess. "It'll take a couple of days to finish."

"Good," he said. "How about you bring Ethan with you tomorrow? While I'm home, that is," he added.

Spinning around, she almost lost her balance. "Bring Ethan? To work?"

"Yeah, I miss the little cuss. And if we're going to be a family, he should be here with us."

"A fa-family?" she stumbled over.

He grinned from ear to ear. "Yes, LizzyBeth, a family. I don't want a fling with you because I want it all."

"But children?"

"I want Ethan and even more with you." It had taken time, but he knew God had his little girl in His hands. There was no reason not to have other children grace this world and bless his life, and he wanted them with LizzyBeth.

"More?" she said.

He couldn't help but chuckle at her stunned surprise and one-to-two-word answers. "Yes, more. Should we start working on one now?"

"But…."

Walking to her, he smiled. "I love you, LizzyBeth. I want you and Ethan to be part of my life."

"But—" she started again.

"But nothing. We'll be a family just as soon as you're ready. Until then, when you come to work here, you bring your son." *Soon to be our son*, he hoped. "What do you say?"

She flung herself into his arms. "Oh, Cowboy. I love you, too. I didn't think you would take us as a family."

The wetness from her tears touched his neck. Why was she crying? "What's wrong?" he asked, pulling her away so he could see her face. "Why are you crying? Did I say something wrong?" Heck, he had never had a steady relationship before this, except for Jasmine. But this—LizzyBeth and Ethan—was right.

"Those are happy tears," she said.

"Does that mean you'll be mine, forever and ever? You

and Ethan?"

"Yes, Cowboy. We'll be yours forever and ever."

About The Author

Sheila Kell writes about the romantic men who leave women's hearts pounding with a happily ever after built on memorable, adrenaline-pumping stories. Or, (since her editor tries to cut down on her long-windedness) simply "Smokin' Hot Romance & Intrigue." Her debut novel, *His Desire* (HIS Series #1), launched as an Amazon #1 romantic suspense bestseller and Top 100 overall, later winning the Readers' Favorite award for best romantic suspense novel.

As a Southern girl who has left behind her days with the United States Air Force and as a University Vice President, she can usually be found nestled in the Mississippi woods, where she lives with her cats and all the strays that magically find her front door. When she isn't writing, you can find Sheila with her nose in a good book, dealing with the woodland critters who enjoy her back porch, or wishing she had a genie to do her bidding.

Sheila is a proud member of Romance Writers of America.

For more information, visit Sheila's website and subscribe to her newsletter: WWW.SHEILAKELLBOOKS.COM

You may also find and follow Sheila on:

FACEBOOK: @SHEILAKELLBOOKS

INSTAGRAM: @SHEILAKELLBOOKS

GOODREADS: @SHEILAKELLBOOKS

BOOKBUB: /AUTHORS/SHEILA-KELL

AMAZON: /AUTHOR/SHEILAKELL

Join Sheila's Facebook Reader Group:
Sheila's Smokin' Hot Heroines

Contact Sheila for information on her advance teams and
other ways to follow: sheila@sheilakell.com

Books by Sheila Kell

Hamilton Investigation & Security: H I S Series

HIS DESIRE

He's stubborn. She's independent. Together, desire will determine their future.

Will his stubbornness prevent him from trusting the woman he desires? In Sheila Kell's provocative novel of suspicion and need, a handsome security specialist and a feisty FBI agent are tied by grief and attraction… and the fervor of the unknown.

HIS CHOICE

Every choice requires a decision, but some choices are determined by the heart.

Will his choice mean certain death to the woman he promised to protect? In Sheila Kell's passionate novel of deception and desire, a smoking-hot enforcer and a determined reporter are destined to make choices that will change everything.

HIS RETURN

Only his return can determine her future.

Will the actions of his past prevent him from returning to the woman in his heart? In Sheila Kell's sensual novel of secrets and unrequited love, a wounded operative, and a strong-willed accountant have to decide if the future can only be determined by the past.

HIS CHANCE

One steamy night in Vegas will change everything.

What happens when one hot night in Vegas irrevocably changes his future? In Sheila Kell's sexy novel of second chances and risks, a red-hot computer nerd and a stubborn ex-FBI agent are drawn together by an undeniable attraction and the chance to save lives.

HIS DESTINY

Despite their secrets, he'll discover she's always been his destiny.

What happens when his destiny leads him into the arms of the woman he doesn't think he deserves? In Sheila Kell's passionate novel of distrust and desire, a damaged man and a broken woman are connected by heartbreak and danger…

and the heat of possibility.

HIS FAMILY

When family stands together anything is possible.

What happens when a man used to being in control has to call in his family to rescue the woman he loves? In Sheila Kell's novella of danger and desire, a charismatic U.S. Senator and an assertive CEO are connected by the love they share. A love about to be ripped out from beneath them.

HIS HEART

His heart is hers.

What happens when a man is called to protect the woman who captured then crushed his heart? In Sheila Kell's story of danger and second chances, two people are connected by a painful past and a love that is threatened.

HIS FANTASY

Fantasies can come true.

Can one man capture the heart of the one woman who walked away from him? In Sheila Kell's novel of conspiracies and desire, a fierce protector refuses to let go of the one complicated woman whose life he feels is threatened.

A HAMILTON CHRISTMAS

While some may try, no one ruins a Hamilton family Christmas.

What happens when a family comes together for Christmas but upon arrival their vacation takes a deadly turn? In Sheila Kell's novel of intrigue and the love of one family, three generations of Hamiltons work to solve a mystery that impacts one of their own.

Agents of H I S Series

EVENING SHADOWS

When deception leads to vengeance, it's only your heart you can trust.

When his life depends on the woman who holds secrets, can he trust their love will be enough for her to seek the truth? In Sheila Kell's thrilling novel of deception and second chances, two operatives embark on a dangerous journey that will test them as agents, friends, and lovers.

MIDNIGHT ESCAPE

When danger hides in plain sight.

What happens when danger is where one least expects it?

In Sheila Kell's thrilling novel of desire and betrayal, a fierce protector and an artist are tied together by a potential threat from thousands of miles away.

AFTERNOON DELIGHT

He's charismatic, and she's cautious.

What happens when a man who solves problems by blowing them up finds himself in a situation where diplomacy is the best plan of attack?

Made in the USA
Columbia, SC
08 October 2024

43296107R00124